trudy

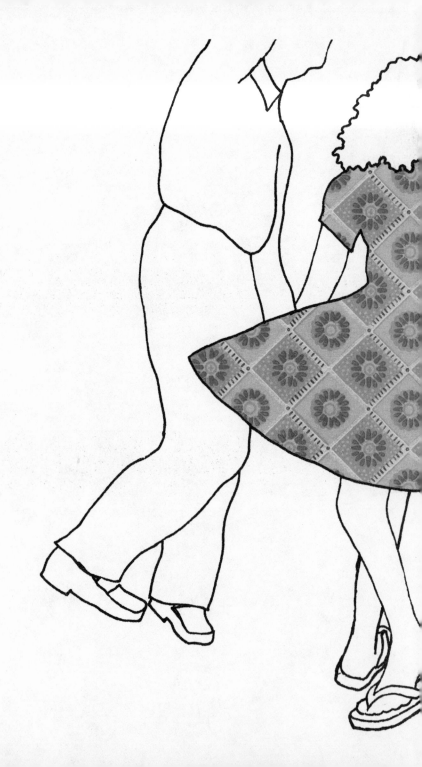

trudy

JESSICA LEE ANDERSON

MILKWEED
EDITIONS

The characters and events in this book are fictitious. Any similarity to real persons, living or dead, is coincidental and not intended by the author.

Published 2005 by Milkweed Editions
Printed in Canada
Cover design and illustration by HartungKemp
Author photo by Tim Kingsbury
Interior design by Dorie McClelland
The text of this book is set in ITC Berkeley.
05 06 07 08 09   5 4 3 2 1
First Edition

Milkweed Editions, a nonprofit publisher, gratefully acknowledges support from Emilie and Henry Buchwald; Bush Foundation; Cargill Value Investment; Timothy and Tara Clark Family Charitable Fund; DeL Corazón Family Fund; Dougherty Family Foundation; Ecolab Foundation; Joe B. Foster Family Foundation; General Mills Foundation; Jerome Foundation; Kathleen Jones; Constance B. Kunin; D.K. Light; Chris and Ann Malecek; McKnight Foundation; a grant from the Minnesota State Arts Board, through an appropriation by the Minnesota State Legislature, a grant from the National Endowment for the Arts, and private funders; Sheila C. Morgan; Laura Jane Musser Fund; an award from the National Endowment for the Arts, which believes that a great nation deserves great art; Navarre Corporation; Kate and Stuart Nielsen; Outagamie Charitable Foundation; Qwest Foundation; Debbie Reynolds; St. Paul Travelers Foundation; Ellen and Sheldon Sturgis; Surdna Foundation; Target Foundation; Gertrude Sexton Thompson Charitable Trust (George R. A. Johnson, Trustee); James R. Thorpe Foundation; Toro Foundation; Weyerhaeuser Family Foundation; and Xcel Energy Foundation.

Library of Congress Cataloging-in-Publication Data

Anderson, Jessica.
  Trudy / Jessica Lee Anderson.— 1st ed.
    p. cm.
  Summary: Twelve-year-old Trudy's life is filled with changes, mainly centered around starting middle school, and as she struggles to take them all in stride she is hit with the biggest change of all—her elderly father's diagnosis of dementia.
  ISBN-13: 978-1-57131-660-8 (hardcover : alk. paper)
  ISBN-10: 1-57131-660-4 (hardcover : alk. paper)
  ISBN-13: 978-1-57131-659-2 (pbk. : alk. paper)
  ISBN-10: 1-57131-659-0 (pbk. : alk. paper)
  [1. Change--Fiction. 2. Old age--Fiction. 3. Middle schools--Fiction. 4.
Family life--Texas—Fiction. 5. Schools--Fiction. 6. Alzheimer's
disease—Fiction. 7. Texas—Fiction.] I. Title.
  PZ7.A53665Tr 2005
  [Fic]--dc22
                        2005008402

J MIDDLE SCHOOL

This book is printed on acid-free paper.

Dedicated to Nana, and to Papa, who has so
lovingly taken care of her.

A special thanks to my husband, Michael,
as well as my parents, friends, and family.
Also, a special thanks to the wonderful folks at
Milkweed who have made this book possible.

Trudy

trudy

Names Can Hurt You

I miss the way things used to be. I miss the days before lockers, class schedules, and losing my best friend, Ashley. We pinky swore that things wouldn't change. But they did.

We used to share slumber parties and talk on the phone about anything. Then anything turned into nothing between us.

Ashley is in honors classes at Benavidez and, well, I'm not. She pointed it out when we talked on the phone the last time we talked as friends, even though she acted like she was kidding.

"Gertrude," she said, "you are just a regular." I cringed. I hate being called Gertrude and I hate being a regular.

Everyone calls me Trudy. My full name is Gertrude Lynn White.

My mother named me after her mother, who died long before I knew about her. I wonder if she felt like I did about my name. It's like glue on my tongue—old sticky glue.

Ms. Gwen's Mistake

Ma and Pop insisted on going to open house. They'd gone all my years in elementary and they just had to visit Benavidez Middle School too.

We'd already been to my social studies class and math class. Mr. Yardley, my math teacher, made sure he showed my parents the *algorithms* we were going to work on during the year. He always uses fancy words like that.

I was especially excited to visit Ms. Gwen—the nicest, and the prettiest, of all my teachers. And she teaches my favorite subject, language arts. When we walked into the classroom, Ms. Gwen's face lit up and her rosy cheeks glowed as she looked at me and my parents. "Trudy, you made it! Are these your grandparents?"

I think she realized right away how stupid her comment had been. At least I hope so.

"No," I said, hating Ms. Gwen for making me go through this again. "They're my parents," I mumbled.

Ma's face became red and blotchy, like someone had pinched her cheeks ten times on each side. The rose in Ms. Gwen's cheeks wilted and turned white. Standing there, Ma and Ms. Gwen were like a candy cane of emotions.

Pop just stood there picking at a scab on his hand from his latest gardening incident. And he was quiet too, like always. He has a way of speaking his concern without saying any words.

"Would you like to see Trudy's portfolio?" Ms. Gwen asked. They both agreed; Ma with a very enthusiastic yes, and Pop with his famous nod. I just sighed and stared at the slightest dot of blood on Pop's hand.

Ma and Pop didn't stay long in Ms. Gwen's class. After we left her room, Ma scratched her scalp and said she was ready to go home. Pop didn't disagree. "She's just young," he said, trying to make Ma feel better.

On the way home I kept telling myself to forgive Ms. Gwen. I suppose it's an easy enough mistake to make. My parents are old. Real old.

The Famous Surprise

The next day at school, Ms. Gwen said to me, "It was a pleasure to meet your parents. Only a few visited this year."

"Thanks Ms. Madison," I said, but she didn't seem to notice my slipup.

I try to learn all my teachers' first names. But Ms. Gwen's last name is like a first name. Her first name is Madison and that's like a last name. Knowing a name means knowing a little more about a person.

I couldn't hold Ms. Madison Gwen's slipup against her, not when a mistake like that is so easy to make. So during lunch I talked to her to make her feel better—to make myself feel better, actually. I've always loved telling the story I told her.

"When my mom went to the doctor, she thought something was wrong. The doctor told her she had a tumor at least the size of a grapefruit. He scheduled all kinds of tests to find out more. Meanwhile, Ma thought she was going to die."

Ms. Gwen looked at me with her kind eyes as I paused at the scary part of the story.

"Well, it wasn't cancer. Ma was pregnant. She was fifty-three years old, too, and Pop was nine years older than her! Ma says she felt like Sarah in the Bible, who was almost a hundred when she had her first baby. Just think, though, Ma was about half Sarah's age when she had me and she was still old."

Ms. Gwen smiled and told me, "For every bad thing, there is usually something good that happens out of it."

Ma says the same thing. I was the good that came out of the cancer scare.

Dancing Lessons and Oatmeal

Pop had an annual checkup with Dr. Modge. The doctor told him that his cholesterol levels were high, especially not the good kind. None of it sounded good to me. Dr. Modge gave him some fancy prescription and told him to eat oatmeal. And get plenty of exercise.

At breakfast time, Ma made oatmeal for everyone. "Just ignore the lumps," she told us, her cheeks red with frustration. Buttons had the right idea and ignored breakfast all together.

Buttons normally filled our empty chair at the table by sitting upright on her haunches, begging. Not that morning—she stayed in the living room, sleeping with her feet straight up in the air in a spot where the sunshine was the warmest.

The oatmeal was the kind you have to cook over a stove, not the instant kind we were used to. We tried adding spoonfuls of brown sugar and milk, but it still tasted bland and felt chunky going down our throats.

"Mighty nice of you to cook breakfast," Pop said to Ma. Then he turned to me and scrunched up his nose and crossed his eyes. My laughs gave him away.

"Oh, don't you tease me." Ma pushed her plate away, then started to smile. "This breakfast certainly ranks up there with some of the worst things I've ever cooked," she said.

Halfway through his bowl of oatmeal, Pop started to laugh. Not a small, whispery laugh, but the kind that comes from the soul, thick and wonderful.

Hearing my father laugh got me laughing so hard I snorted. We were a trio of laughing bells ringing. Buttons jumped to her feet and ran into the kitchen, unable to ignore breakfast any longer.

In the pan, the gross mush had started to harden. Pop told us to follow him as he took the pan outside. Ma and I hurried after him, Buttons barking with nearly every step we took.

When I got to the porch, I spied Pop hiding behind the green hawthorn he had planted for me when I was born. I could see his white shirt through all the clusters of red berries. His head peeked out from behind the trunk.

I heard him laugh, and then I saw a bomb of oatmeal flying at me. I didn't have a chance to duck before I felt the "whap" where it landed on my arm.

"Tag!" he yelled. He tried throwing a ball of oatmeal at Ma, but he missed. Ma immediately leaped over to him, scooped out some oatmeal, and dumped it on his head. Buttons sniffed at what fell on the ground. She didn't dare eat it. The oatmeal was gone before I had a chance to hit Pop back.

"Well," Pop said as he wiped oatmeal away from his face, "eating oatmeal isn't going to work, but maybe I can start to exercise." He laughed again, his laugh thicker than the clump of oatmeal on his head.

Then he promised to teach me how to dance that day.

Clearing the Patio

Ma bent over to move a chair off the patio and, just like in the cartoons, her jeans button popped clear off. Ma dug her fingers into her hair and scowled. But instead of getting upset, she pushed her stomach in and out until it began to roll like a wave.

"I suppose it will make it easier to dance now," Ma said, patting her ocean of a stomach. "I certainly didn't have a body like this when your daddy and I learned to dance. It's been a long time." She gazed off beyond the fence like it was yesterday. "That was how your daddy stole my heart. I have never seen a man with faster feet."

I tried imagining that, but I couldn't. Pop walks with a shuffle—he never seems concerned about hurrying. "Don't know what the big rush is," he always says.

"Before the war, your father and I would dance the night away. Even after that, but it took him some time to heal," Ma said, moving the grill onto the grass. I moved the chairs to the edge of the patio.

My father was in World War II and he was a hero. He never talked about it much, but as a soldier in France he laid communication lines on the ground. He also detected land mines. But there was one he didn't detect—the one that he stepped on. He lost part of his right leg and even part of his behind. Pins and time put him back together again

But after that, Ma told me in secret, he never talked as much.

Learning to Waltz

Pop tried showing me the waltz, but there were too many steps to learn. It was like too many numbers in math class. Buttons ran wildly around our feet, biting at our heels.

"Geez," I fussed after I tripped over Pop's feet again and came close to kicking Buttons. She scooted away from me with her tail pinned down like I'd hurt her feelings. "Sorry, girl," I whispered to her.

"I'm never going to learn," I whined.

"Am I that bad a teacher?" Pop asked. "Don't try so hard," he coached.

I let the numbers slip out of my head and focused on how Pop's skinny arms held me tight as he whirled me around. I looked up in the sky and all I could see was motion. A blur of motion.

Even though I tripped over his feet again and almost cried out in frustration, Pop kissed me on the cheek and whispered, "Thank you for this dance. I hope I didn't let you down." I smiled back at him, hoping he wouldn't guess how much I thought I'd let him down.

Pop then asked Ma to dance and she held out her hand. He kissed it and grabbed her around the waist. His arm fit into the indentation around her middle. The zipper of her jeans flapped open slightly.

The music on the portable boom box faded in and out, but Ma and Pop didn't seem to care. They seemed to be dancing to their own music, filling the gaps with music they'd always known. Buttons quit her scurrying and sat back with me to watch them dance, witnessing the same sort of magic.

The peppered hair of my father and the yellow-white hair of my mother danced along with their full bodies. It was hard to tell who was who. Around and around they went, blending together as they whirled.

Conjectures and Tears

"What did you get?" Imelda Ghoelke leaned over and asked after Ms. Gwen passed our essays back. I cupped my hand over the scribble at the top of the page.

"Hope it's nothing bad," I answered as I looked down. "What about you?" I asked Imelda. I looked back at my essay. I ran my finger secretly over the letter A and Ms. Gwen's note that read, "Trudy, you are an artist with language."

"Worse than you probably," Imelda joked. "You're the biggest nerd I know."

I wish all my classes were like Ms. Gwen's. History isn't bad and neither is science, but there is something special about Madison Gwen's class.

PE is a terror—I don't want people to see me undressing. Math is the worst, though. I don't think Mr. Yardley gets it that we don't get it. He talks so fast and gives a quiz at the end of every period. I made a thirteen on the last one. I just don't get it.

We were working on a number series yesterday, a series full of patterns. He called on me to come up with a conjecture. A conjecture?

"Five," I said, the same number of letters in the word s–h–a–m–e. The whole class laughed at me and I watched Kim Ledesma lean over to one of her friends and whisper something, probably something about what an idiot I am.

Mr. Yardley lost his usual smile and shouted, "If you would take this class more seriously, Gertrude, you wouldn't get a thirteen on your quiz!" He was so mad at me.

I'd answered seriously. I tried holding back my tears. They tasted sad and angry in my throat. My ears burned from the pressure. The tears came anyway.

I am an artist with language. Not numbers.

A Conference of Interest

Mr. Yardley called my parents to schedule a conference.

"He says your mathematical capabilities aren't up to par," Ma said, lifting her eyebrow like she wanted some sort of explanation. "Trudy, are there things you aren't telling us about?" She put down her crocheting and looked at me.

"No, I'm just having a hard time."

"How can we help if there are things we don't know about?" Ma fussed.

I shrugged my shoulders.

Pop decided not to go to the conference. He preferred pulling weeds and getting new cuts and scratches to picking at his old ones out of nervousness.

It was weird seeing Ma after school, because Pop was the one who usually picked me up. She gave me a quick wave when she saw me.

Ma and I were both quiet as we walked to Mr. Yardley's room. I could feel sweat pooling in my armpits.

There was a strong armpit smell, too, a smell I felt proud of somehow. A mark of the transition Ma keeps talking about.

Mr. Yardley greeted Ma and wasted no time before showing her my quiz score and some of my other bad grades. All of them actually.

Ma's lips were tight, but I couldn't tell if she was mad at me or not.

"Mrs. White, grades don't really matter, but Trudy doesn't seem to have a solid mathematical foundation. I'm thinking of taking Trudy out of the regular classroom and getting her placed in Resource."

I sat there, invisible to both Ma and Mr. Yardley.

"Resource?" Ma asked. Her face looked more wrinkled than ever before.

"Where she can get the extra help she needs," Mr. Yardley tried to explain.

Ma wasn't so quiet when she said, "Well, I guess grades DO matter when you're failing my daughter. And you're failing too when a student fails to succeed. Trudy is a smart girl. I don't agree with pulling Trudy out of her class. She should be with her peers in a normal setting."

My sweat dripped down my sides. Warm and cool at the same time.

"Give her a chance, Mr. Yardley," Ma continued.

"I'll think of something, Mrs. White, a plan to scaffold Trudy's mathematical understandings. But please understand that the next step is Resource."

"Fine." Ma stood up and shook his hand, her lips still stretched in a thin line.

"In my opinion, that teacher of yours could use some strong scaffolding," Ma said as we left the school, and she struck her hands together, making a loud slapping noise.

If Imelda knew about Mr. Yardley's meeting she'd think twice about calling me a nerd. A nerd wouldn't be failing math.

Possibilities

Ma stuck her head into my room. "I'm going to the craft store for some more yarn. Want to come?" she asked.

"No, thanks."

"Your father is outside in his shop in case you need anything," she said.

The door to the greenhouse was shut. Through the clear walls, I could see Pop slumped over in his chair.

"Pop!" I screamed again and again. Buttons barked as loud as I yelled and scratched on the door in a frenzy. "Pop!" I pushed the door open and shook Pop's shoulder.

"Shh," Pop whispered as he lifted his head. Plants of every shape and size filled the space around him. "Shh." He sat upright and covered something in his hands. I could feel my legs giving out—first from fear, then from relief.

"I'm all right," he said. I must've looked like I didn't believe him. I could feel my heart beating so powerfully that all the veins in my body pounded.

The light inside the greenhouse made his face look like an old painting. "I wanted to surprise you," he told me.

Pop placed his surprise in my hands. Looking down I found a bulb of some kind. My fingers traced along the dirty, layered edges. I didn't say anything.

"I meant to plant it," Pop held up a brown pot filled with soil, "but I must've fallen asleep."

"What kind of bulb is it? Is it a lily or a tulip?"

Pop shrugged his shoulders. "Planting it will tell."

"Thank you," I told him. I let the bulb lie in the palm of my hand.

"Just think of the joy it will bring," he said. "Like my daughter."

Ashley, the Tutor

Mr. Yardley had a talk with me before I went to lunch. Since I hadn't said anything at the conference, I tried to explain that I wasn't trying to be funny about the conjecture.

"Your grades, Trudy, are not a funny matter either," Mr. Yardley said.

"I try so hard, Mr. Yardley." I felt uncomfortable being in the room with him alone. He was so serious with me. His first name is Bartholomew. I smiled as I remembered his name. He didn't seem so serious to me that way.

"I want your grades to improve, Trudy. I'd like to think you can do the work, but you may not be trying hard enough." I let out a big sigh. If he only knew the truth. Inside my head, I could hear Pop's voice saying, "Don't try so hard."

"I'm picking some students out of this class to be tutored by the honors class. I think you could benefit from this, Trudy. If not, you know the repercussions."

At first, I didn't know what to think about it. I wanted to be better at math, but having a tutor meant I was stupid. I tried not to think that way, but I felt like dumb had been stamped across my forehead. Dumb and nerd have the same number of letters.

"You'll be working with Ashley Sanchez after school if you agree to it."

As soon as he said it, I imagined how different things could be. I smiled inside so Mr. Yardley couldn't tell how excited I was and change his mind. Something positive out of something bad?

Tutoring

I felt restless all day. I kept thinking that working with Ashley might bring us closer again. I imagined how perfect things were going to be. I waited for tutoring, but somehow I didn't want it to come, either.

I went to Mr. Yardley's room after school. Ashley was already there. So were other people getting tutored. Kim Ledesma looked up at me with eyes so intense they seemed to say, "You better not tell anyone you saw me here."

Mr. Yardley walked up to me. "Take out your homework, Trudy, and ask Ashley any questions you have."

I rolled my eyes behind Mr. Yardley's back, but Ashley didn't laugh. She would have last year. There's a seriousness to life at Benavidez, a wall that seems impossible to climb sometimes.

I looked down at my homework to avoid her staring eyes—eyes that said she didn't want to be there. My paper was blank.

I took out my math book and looked at the problem. I wrote it out on my paper, checking my paper and then the book, the book and then my paper. I was stalling for time. I didn't want Ashley to see how dumb I felt.

"Twenty-four."

"Huh?"

"The answer is twenty-four," Ashley snapped, as if in a hurry. To get away from me? I looked over at Kim to see if she was hearing this, but she was looking down.

"I don't want the answer, Ash. I think it's important for me to learn myself," I whispered.

"I don't think you can. Don't call me Ash anymore, Gertrude!" she yelled. I'm sure everyone heard, including Kim. I couldn't take what she said. I got up and walked slowly out the door and then ran down the hallway so no one would see how much Ashley had upset me.

I was grateful to see Pop waiting for me in the station wagon outside. He gave me a nod, then reached over and opened the door like he did every day.

"I wasn't sure what happened," Pop said. I could see the worry in his face.

"Why?" I asked.

"I kept waiting for you."

"Did you forget I had tutoring today?"

"I must've," he said. Pop and I seemed to let out a long sigh together.

White Weekend Lie

Weekends came and went, but I didn't look forward to them like I used to. I could predict exactly what they were going to be like. Weekends felt like a bad habit.

I planted my mystery bulb and watered it. I kept watching for the soil to reveal the secret, but nothing changed.

Everything else seemed to change, though, especially with Ma and Pop. Pop used to clank around the kitchen and surprise us with cakes and casseroles. He would grow the most beautiful flowers and take them to neighbors. And Ma used to have this energy about her, like the time she painted half the house before I got home from school. She didn't get so frustrated then and Pop wasn't so tired.

I walked into the living room to see what Ma and Pop were doing. One look at Pop gave me the answer. Nothing. He was asleep on the couch with his mouth wide open. He still had dirt underneath his fingernails from working in his garden. Buttons was curled in a ball near his feet, snoring just slightly less.

Ma had a crochet hook in her hand and a pile of fuzzy yarn in her lap.

"Why do you have to crochet all the time?" I asked her.

"I like to make things just like your father likes to grow things. Besides, it helps my hands." Ma's hands had started crippling years ago from rheumatoid arthritis. Once when she'd pointed straight out in the distance at a deer, Pop and I looked to the right, following the bend of her crooked finger.

I ached to hang out with Ashley, but when I picked up the phone to call her, I couldn't. I thought about all the other people I could call, but it made the phone feel even more silent. I felt so alone.

Saturday was fun as we waltzed the time away, even though Ma and Pop did most of the dancing. But Sunday left me with a feeling of dread.

I didn't want another week to begin. After Ma and Pop tucked me in on Sunday night, a habit that never seemed worth breaking, sleep wouldn't come. I tried. I rolled. I covered my head with a pillow. Nothing.

I went to the bathroom and pretended to throw up. I made a bunch of noise to be sure I'd be heard.

Ma rushed in after I flushed an empty toilet. She took my temperature and gave me some Pepto-Bismol. She hummed a song that sounded like "Silent Night." Her humming reminded me of being held close when she used to rock me to sleep. Back and forth we would glide. Sleep finally came.

Ma, the Could-Have-Been Veterinarian

"We can hire you a tutor," Ma said. She checked over my shoulder to make sure I was working on my math problems.

"We can't afford that," I told her, but I hoped I wasn't right. Pop retired a few years before I was born and Ma retired when she found out she was pregnant. Money has always been tight for us.

"Maybe we can find a hungry scholar we can pay with home-cooked meals," Ma joked.

I raised my eyebrows in question.

"OK, maybe not my home cooking," Ma said with a laugh. Pop used to be the main cook, but then he forgot his recipes—the ones he never wrote down. And then one day he got distracted when he was frying some chicken and started a small fire.

"I'd help you if I could," Ma said. "If I was in your

class that teacher of yours would want to scaffold the tar out of me."

Ma didn't go to school past the eighth grade. She was the oldest of seven children and was expected to take care of the younger ones. Things were much different on a farm in Vermont in her day.

"I wanted to be a veterinarian, Trudy, but there was just too much work to catch up on." I looked over at Buttons and remembered how Ma had fed her as a stray and then nursed her back to health.

Most dogs named Buttons are named that because they have a cute button nose. Not our dog, though, not at first anyway. She had mange so bad it looked like button sores were sewed on to her skin. But it wasn't long before Ma had that terrier so healthy you couldn't help but notice her button nose.

"I don't know, Trudy, it just never happened. I liked working in the office, though, and I love being your daddy's wife. I love being your mother best of all."

Ma looked out the window again, still searching for yesterday.

"Gertrude, I don't want you to fall in the same trap I did. Be strong in all the ways I wasn't. Don't let your education slip like I did."

The way Ma says my name, I feel proud to be her Gertrude.

Roshanda's Gift

"You always eat your lunch alone," a girl named Roshanda said as she sat down next to me in the court-yard. "Does it ever bother you?" she asked, her eyes brown and big.

I could feel myself stuttering before I answered her. Everyone calls her Tower because she's so tall and sturdy like a tree.

"Sometimes," I answered. "What about you?" I dared to ask.

"Being alone all the time?" Roshanda opened her lunch bag. "I guess I like my reputation," she said with a smile that didn't seem to match her tough, towering image. She pulled out a smashed sandwich.

"To be honest," she said, "I like being left alone. Things are so noisy at home I guess I like it quiet at school."

"I'm kind of the opposite. Sometimes it just gets way too quiet at home," I told her as I watched her peel the plastic from her bread.

"I heard what that girl Ashley said to you in tutoring. Don't let her get you down."

"Thanks."

We talked through lunch and, that easily, I made a new friend.

"I could help you out with math sometime," Roshanda offered.

"I promise I'll be quiet," I told her. She laughed and put her strong branch of an arm on my shoulder, sealing the deal of our new friendship.

I told Pop about her when he picked me up after school.

Studying with Ro-Ro

My promise to be quiet was quickly broken. When Roshanda and I studied math together for the first time, I learned how good she is with numbers. And, for someone called Tower, she isn't as serious as you'd imagine.

With each problem we solved, we made fun of Mr. Yardley's way of talking.

"You have this six and you extrimicanate the number and then you conjoinayoin. Can you conjectricate?"

It doesn't sound so funny now, but I could hardly stop laughing. I could see Imelda staring at us from across the cafeteria.

Roshanda told me that even with his big words, Mr. Yardley still couldn't get some things straight. He'd been calling Roshanda Rhonda since school started.

"I try correcting that man all the time, but he just don't seem to listen. Names are always getting me in trouble. Even my little brother at home slipped and called me Tower."

"At least Tower sounds like a good strong name. Last year at our church retreat, I heard a rumor that everyone was calling me Gertrude-the-Nerdy-Prude."

Roshanda had to clap her hand over her mouth to keep the laughs from falling out.

"They should've been calling you Trudy Booty," Roshanda said, her laughs escaping.

"Oh! You didn't, Ro-Ro," I said, and looked over my shoulder at my behind. We both laughed so hard that not just Imelda Ghoelke was staring at us. The nicknames stuck. Ro-Ro and Trudy Booty.

Changes

"Trudy, have you heard from Ashley lately?" Ma asked after school, her hands working a ball of yarn with her crochet hook. When she looked up at me, her hands kept right on hooking and knotting.

"That couch throw is coming along," I answered. I didn't want to talk about it.

Ma's hands quit crocheting and waited for me to give her the real answer.

"Well, she isn't the same, Ma, but I have a new friend. We study math together, so you don't have to worry about paying for a tutor. Better yet, you don't have to worry about cooking." I smiled after I said it because we really haven't studied much.

"People change, especially around the transition. Tell me about your friend," Ma said.

So I told her about Ro-Ro, though I didn't tell her about my nickname.

"Have you talked to Pop lately?" Ma asked, interrupting our conversation. I hadn't even told her the things we said about Mr. Yardley.

"Not really," I said. I didn't tell her about Pop's gift. "Why?"

"He's been so quiet lately," Ma said.

"Pop's always quiet."

Ma shrugged her shoulders, and her hands went back to hooking and knotting.

"He just seems so different," Ma added as her hands continued to hook and then knot.

Run-Ins

In the morning, I bumped into Ashley in the hall. She brushed off her shoulder like she was cleaning off germs. Maybe it was a bad sign.

Changing into my gym clothes in PE, I wasn't as careful as usual. Instead of going into a bathroom stall, I just took my shirt off quickly, figuring I wouldn't be noticed. Not a chance.

Kim shouted when she saw me: "Oh my God, what happened to you?"

Then every other girl in the locker room turned and stared at my chest. Not at my cream and white lace bra, but at my skin.

A girl named Latrice said, "You look like a trussed-up turkey!"

"I feel like one with all of you staring!" My scar felt private. My own little secret of my fragile past. "Stop staring at me!"

Kim pressed on, "Well, what happened?"

I told them then. I'd practiced before what I would say in case there was a run-in.

"My mother had a difficult pregnancy. She didn't know if I was ever going to be able to come into the world. Her heart ached at the thought of losing me and I guess the heartache passed along. I was born with congenital heart problems. Surgery fixed the problem, but they had to cut my chest all the way open."

Nobody said anything after that. No questions. No comments. Not such a big deal. To them at least.

Images and Pains in the Chest

When I bought my first bra, Ma went in the dressing room with me. "I was close to sixteen when my mother bought me my first bra," she said.

Ma looked at the scars on my chest and told me it looked like they'd faded since she saw them last. I didn't think so, but Ma always tried to be encouraging.

Ma helped fit me into a cream bra with white lace. "Your body is going to be changing, Trudy. Many girls your age start having a negative body image. Be proud of who you are, Miss White."

Not too soon after that talk, Ma had to worry about her own body image. Her doctors found a lump in her breast. Two actually. They removed both lumps, and now Ma says she has one full sized boob and one that "looks like it's in training."

"I always hoped I'd grow more," Ma said, looking down at her chest after her surgery. She pinched her stomach instead. "Now I'd do anything to stop growing."

It wasn't cancer, but it still changed her.

Soon after she healed, we went and bought a new bra for her. A sports bra, so the size of the cups didn't matter. Cream, like my first bra.

Walking the Dog

After Pop drove me home from school, I knew he'd be doing one of two things—either snoring on the couch or working outside with his plants. But then he started sleeping more than gardening. Garden magazines still arrived in the mail, but Pop just stacked them in the den, unread.

One day after we'd been home awhile, I noticed that he had caked mud all over himself. And Buttons had mud worked into her coarse fur.

"What have you been working on?" I asked him.

"I can't remember," he said.

We were no longer dancing much, either. Pop said his legs had been hurting and Ma made the same complaint. The weather had started to get colder, too.

"Trudy, how about we take walks together instead?" Pop suggested.

"With Buttons?" I asked. I should've known—that dog is like Velcro connected to him.

I didn't want to tell him that I wasn't wild about dancing in the first place. I don't have the rhythm or the patience. I just liked spending time with him. Sometimes it was just pulling weeds with him in the backyard—me in one corner of the yard and him on the other side.

On our first walk, Pop didn't speak. We walked together, side by side, Pop's feet shuffling and Buttons' toenails tapping on the sidewalk. I could hear Pop breathing heavy even though we didn't go far. Or very fast.

The Warm Cool Front

The same day that we had the coldest cool front in the month of October, we got a new student in Ms. Gwen's class.

Jerome Becker—with crystal blue eyes and the fullest lips I'd ever seen. I can't remember much else about him, except those eyes and lips.

"Welcome to Benavidez," was all I said to him when he said hello. I thought of many things to say after.

"Thanks," was Jerome's response. Did his eyes sparkle brighter?

"My name is Trudy. It's freezing here today. Austin usually isn't this cold. Especially in October."

"Trudy, this is hot where I come from. I could wear shorts and be fine! This place is nothing like Michigan."

"So what brings you here?"

"Gonna live with my dad for a while," he answered, without offering anything more. I certainly didn't have the courage to ask anything else.

I tried looking away, but I had to have another look at those eyes—there was something about them that made me want to keep looking.

The Trouble with Fathers

Ro-Ro has three younger brothers. She's so busy helping her mom that homework doesn't always get finished. She never missed our lunchtime "tutoring," though.

We usually talked and got off task, but I soon noticed that my grades were going up. So did Mr. Yardley.

"Trudy, what have you been doing? Your grades have improved drastically from the first six weeks. Keep it up." Yes, Mr. Yardley, I intend to.

I told Ro-Ro what Mr. Yardley said. She does so many good things, but her teachers don't notice. They only see that she doesn't get her homework done. They don't even ask why.

I also told her about Jerome's blue eyes. She nicknamed him Jerome LaComb.

What Ro-Ro said after we stopped laughing surprised me. "I want nothing to do with boys. They're nothing but trouble!"

She got real quiet and, for a moment, her face looked like a raisin, all scrunched up. Tears welled up in her eyes. The Tower seemed to crumble.

I tried, but I couldn't figure it out. When she stopped to breathe, her watery eyes reflected the pain. "My stepdad left two weeks ago."

I was sure she meant for good. I knew she'd never met her real dad, but her stepdad might as well have been him.

"And this week Mama found out she's pregnant again."

"Does your stepdad know?" I asked.

"Not yet," Ro-Ro said. "But I guess he'll find out he's going to be a father again sooner or later." With her sad eyes, Ro-Ro looked at me and said, "I am never gonna fall in love."

I gave her a hug and told her I'd be there if she needed to talk.

After school, I waited out by the front courtyard, but I didn't see Pop anywhere. I waited and waited some more. Close to an hour went by and there was still no Pop.

Finally, I went to the office and asked to use the phone to call home. After three rings, Pop answered.

"Hello?" he said.

"Where are you? Please, come pick me up!" I yelled into the phone.

The Green Hawthorn

I was relieved when the station wagon finally turned the corner, but I was still upset with Pop.

"How could you forget me?" I asked after he reached over and opened my door.

He shrugged his shoulders. "Sorry," he mumbled.

I didn't say anything else to him as we rode home.

"How was your day at school?" Ma asked when we got back.

"Fine!" I fussed. "Why don't you ask Pop?" I stormed outside and sat on the back porch. Buttons scratched on the door, and when I got up to let her out, Ma was standing there.

"What's going on?" she asked as she came outside to sit with me. Buttons took off running in the yard.

I told her what had happened and how sick to my stomach I'd felt waiting for a Pop who never showed up.

"It's easy to forget things," Ma said, "especially at our age."

"But he's picked me up for as long as I can remember," I said. I watched as a group of sparrows flew around the branches of the green hawthorn.

"Please don't be upset with him. I'll start picking you up," she promised. Her eyes followed the birds as they jumped from twig to twig.

"Pop planted that after you were born," she reminded me. "He wanted to plant a rosebush in honor of his daughter, but when we realized how sick you were, he chose something that grew wild. Your daddy figured if he could get that plant to grow, you would make it just fine."

Ma stopped talking and looked at me. "It started out as an overgrown shrub," her voice softened. "Now it's a tree."

Buttons began to bark at the fence. I watched as the birds flew away. I knew I couldn't be upset with Pop for long.

Pop and Laura Bell

The weather was cool, even though it warmed up some after the front passed. Pop and I went on our evening walk while Ma stayed home to crochet.

"What are you going to do with all the throws you've made?" I asked her before Pop and I went outside.

"I guess they're for someday," Ma said, her eyes full of promise. Ma always talks about things for later—wills, furniture, college, weddings . . .

Pop's walking had slowed down even more and he seemed less in a rush than ever. "Are you doing OK, Pop?" I asked.

He smiled at me, a confused smile, and simply nodded his head up and down. I didn't know a quiet man could become even quieter.

"What would you say to a friend who's going through something pretty bad?" I asked him, but he didn't answer. He looked down at Buttons. He looked like he was trying to solve the problems of the world.

"Pop, she's so smart, but she has such bad grades."
When I talked about Ro-Ro, though, I felt bad that I
could walk with my father while her father was no
longer there.

As we walked back down Dutch Avenue toward
home, Pop reached for my hand and said, "I love you,
Laura Bell."

Laura Bell?

Heart Problems and Heartaches

I kept wondering if Laura Bell was a nickname Pop had given me. Thinking about it was burning a hole in my mind. I decided to ask Ma.

"Ma, who is Laura Bell?" She looked at me for a long minute, her face all twisted as she tried to straighten out her thoughts.

"Your father had a sister who was about your age when she died," Ma said quietly. "He only talked about her a few times. You could tell how much it hurt him. I think he felt guilty that there was nothing he could do to save her. He was like a father to her."

"How did she die, Ma?"

"She was born with heart problems similar to yours, Trudy. She had several surgeries, but the technology wasn't the same as it is now. She was never able to fully recover. Your grandma showed me pictures of her and your father growing up. They seemed very close. Your grandma said you looked just like her as a baby."

I tried taking it all in. I tried imagining Pop growing up with Laura Bell in the small logging town in California. My Pop, full of so many hurts and secrets.

"What makes you ask? Did Pop say something?"

I nodded like Pop does. It wasn't really a yes nod, but it wasn't a no nod either. I didn't want to tell her he'd called me Laura Bell.

An Invitation of Importance

At lunch, I was going to tell Ro-Ro about Laura Bell, but I decided to keep it a secret. Like Pop had kept it from me.

In a way, I felt jealous of Laura Bell. Pop had been so close to her.

Sharing a piece of pizza, Ro-Ro and I talked about Halloween. It was a week and a half away and we had no idea what to be.

"Do you think we're too old to dress up this year?" I asked Ro-Ro.

"You're kidding, right? The older you get, the better the costumes are," she said. She pulled off a greasy chunk of pepperoni and sucked it down.

We were interrupted when Jerome LaComb came and sat with us.

I couldn't say anything. My tongue was glued down. Stapled actually.

Those eyes.

"Are you both going to the Halloween dance?" LaComb asked kind of shyly, his eyes sparkling.

"We haven't thought about it," Ro-Ro said in a strong voice. I was glad she spoke for both of us. But then I worried that Ro-Ro sounded too strong and I seemed too weak.

"Well, my cousin Kenneth and I are going. Maybe we could meet up," Jerome suggested. I could feel myself start shaking with nerves.

"Yeah," I told him as quickly as I could manage so I wouldn't lose my courage. I felt Ro-Ro's foot kick me under the table. But she never complained about me dragging her into it.

A Tale of Two Princesses

For Halloween, I decided to be a spider princess. Ma sewed me a long black dress with see-through fabric sleeves covered with spiderweb designs. Ma was ironing the dress when Ro-Ro arrived. Buttons immediately ran to her and rolled over on her back so Ro-Ro could pet her belly.

Ro-Ro was going to braid my hair before the dance and I was going to put on her makeup.

Pop met her at the door and asked, "Can I get you anything?"

She shook her head no. "But thank you."

We went into my bedroom and Ro-Ro brushed my hair so much that the curls left and a big poof remained. It felt good having her hands in my hair as she gathered strands together.

My hair was half braided when we went into the kitchen.

Pop got out of his seat and asked, "Can I get you anything?"

"No, Pop, we got it."

We grabbed some cheddar crackers and went back to my room. We were to meet Jerome and Kenneth at 7:00 and it was almost 6:15.

We decided to keep my hair half braided in neat rows and the other half wild. I put on my crown, which was painted black.

"How do you want me to do your makeup?" I asked Ro-Ro. I was armed with cotton swabs and Ma's makeup kit.

"Make me look like something other than the Tower," she said. Then she took out her outfit. A white dress. Ro-Ro was going to be a princess bride. I placed the tiara on her already curled hair.

Two princesses, one in black and the other in white.

Ma rushed in with my outfit and got her keys out to drive us to the dance.

Before we left, Pop once again asked Ro-Ro, "Can I get you anything?" Like a broken record.

The Moby Dick Letdown

I had the jitters during our ride to the dance. I closed my eyes and tried to imagine how wonderful it was going to be. Romantic, like poetry in action.

Ro-Ro's dress was beautiful. She'd found it at a thrift store, for not much money. The bride who wore the dress before her must have been tall.

I felt pretty too, even with black lipstick and my hair half in rows, half fro. We arrived early.

After standing near the punch awhile, Ro-Ro spotted Jerome, who was dressed as a hobo. Walking over with him was a guy about two inches taller than Jerome, wearing a suit and a tall hat. I was nervous, and I could tell that Ro-Ro was too. She pinched my elbow and whispered, "Trudy Booty."

Jerome walked up to us and introduced Kenneth.

"What grade are you in?" Kenneth asked Ro-Ro.

She smiled and quietly said, "Sixth." I've never known Ro-Ro to be shy. Kenneth handed her a balloon he'd untied from the back of a chair and got her some punch. As they walked off toward the dance floor, I could smell the trail of his cologne.

Jerome grabbed a balloon once we were alone, and I thought he was going to give it to me. Instead, he untied it and sucked out the helium.

"Why is your hair like that?" Jerome's voice was squeaky as he pointed at my mop.

I shrugged my shoulders. He didn't get me any punch.

More people had arrived, but the boys were on one side and the girls on the other. A few people were dancing. Kenneth and Ro-Ro joined them when the next song started. People from both sides of the room were watching the two of them. I wondered if they even recognized Roshanda. The Tower.

With Kenneth and Ro-Ro gone, Jerome and I stood next to each other awkwardly.

He told me his dog has a Moby Dick eye.

"I'm not sure, but I think it means that one eye is blue and the other is brown," he added. I tried to smile as though I cared, but the dance wasn't turning out at all like I'd imagined.

Marked with a K

Ro-Ro started to go out with Kenneth after Halloween. Ro-Ro, the person who was never going to fall in love. Ro-Ro, the princess bride. Ro-Ro Roshanda Johnson, also known as Tower and sometimes Rhonda.

In Ms. Gwen's class, we drew names for a partner in making a poster about a story we'd read. I drew Jerome's name. I didn't feel as excited as I would have before. Jerome wasn't who I'd wanted him to be.

"Want to work on the project at my house?" he asked. "My dad isn't going to be home."

"No," I answered, feeling like Gertrude-the-Nerdy-Prude. "I have all my stuff at my house."

Ma and Pop didn't seem to care when I mentioned that I'd invited him over.

After meeting my parents, he said, "Your parents are cotton tops."

Anger burned in the back of my eyes as I looked at him.

"They aren't that old," I argued, even though I knew it was a lie.

We worked on our poster in the kitchen. Dad offered him candy at least five times. Ma made sure to leave us alone.

As I added the finishing touches with my marker, Jerome leaned over and kissed me. My first kiss. Sloppy and wet.

Jerome and I got an eighty on the assignment. Not good, but not bad.

Two weeks after the kiss, Jerome moved back to Michigan to live with his mother. Not good, but not bad. I'll miss those eyes more than I'll miss him. As Ma always likes to say, "What's meant to be will be."

Assignments and Losses

Day by day things seemed to get busier. The teachers kept piling on work. Social studies report. Personal narrative. Lab write-ups. Tests. Tests. Tests.

But all the school stress seemed to disappear when Ma got the phone call telling us that Pop's best friend had died. Uncle Frank. I had always called him Uncle Frank, even though he wasn't a relative.

"Trudy," she said, as I got close to her, "Uncle Frank is gone."

Ma was standing beside the car waiting for me when I got out of school.

"Gone where?" I asked, not really sure what she meant. Uncle Frank traveled all over the place.

"He died this afternoon, Trudy." Ma grabbed my fingers, her hand strong and warm in mine. I was so shocked I could focus only on Ma's arms hugging me tight.

"He had a heart attack," Ma said. I couldn't help but think that heart problems surround my family.

We got in the car and headed for home.

"Have you told Pop yet?" I asked.

"No, he was outside watering his plants when the call came. I haven't had the heart to tell him just yet."

Pop was washing his hands at the kitchen sink when we got home. As he dried them on a towel, Ma sat him down and gave him a glass of water.

"Frank died this afternoon." She said it very softly.

Pop just stared at Ma. I couldn't tell how he was taking it.

"Who's Frank?" Pop asked.

My eyes felt big looking at Pop. He looked so old to me at that moment. Deep-canyon wrinkles and a lost look on his face.

With her own eyes wide, Ma explained to Pop, "Frank. Frank DeLong. You grew up with him in Crescent City. You fought together in France."

Pop stared at Ma, then looked at the dirt under his nails.

Shaking some, Ma left the kitchen and came back with a photo album. She showed Pop a picture of Frank in his uniform.

"Was it a land mine?"

Ma shook her head from side to side. "No. He had a heart attack."

Pop began to tear up and Ma's eyes filled with tears too.

Only she couldn't stop. I wondered if they were crying for different reasons.

Making the Most of It

That afternoon, I kept thinking about Uncle Frank being gone. Gone as in dead. Most of Frank's history came before I was born. But all those Christmas days we spent together. I was a flower girl at his second wedding. He wrote me a yearly birthday card.

He meant so much to Pop. A large part of his past, a smaller part of his present, and a future gone. Gone as in dead.

I kept repeating that to myself.

Ma was still kind of tearful, but she'd decided to make the most of Uncle Frank's passing. Something good out of the bad. We were driving to the funeral in Alpine, out in west Texas, and Ma wanted to fit Big Bend National Park into the trip too.

"I always thought it would be nice to take a road trip there someday. We can make someday now," Ma said. "You're going to miss school anyway. We'll just count this as a cultural experience." She looked both sad and mischievous. Her brown eyes looked deep and shiny, even though they were still puffy.

"What about Buttons?" I asked.

"She'll come too. She needs to get away just as much."

To leave enough time for the trip and the funeral, Ma decided we would have to leave at 6:30 in the morning.

Pop nodded his head but added, "Don't know what the big hurry is."

"I want plenty of time to see the park," Ma said.

On the Road

"How long are you going to be gone?" Ro-Ro asked the night before we left on our trip.

"I don't know—it doesn't matter," I answered.

"What do you mean? Of course it does," she said, so loud that she seemed very much the Tower.

"You have Kenneth now."

"Oh, please," Ro-Ro said. "You're the first real friend I've made and that means something. Don't give me that. Be safe and you better send me a letter while you're gone."

That evening, Ma and I went to the grocery store and bought piles of snacks. Chips. Granola. Beef jerky. Trucking food. When we came home, Buttons gave all the bags a good inspection.

I made sure the gift Pop gave me got a thorough watering. I was still waiting for a tulip or something to appear, but nothing was growing yet.

When we started loading up the car, Pop asked, "Where are we going again?"

Ma just shook her head and explained once again the reason for our trip.

It was hard getting up in the morning, but we managed to hit the road at 6:36 AM, only six minutes past our goal.

"Not bad. Not bad," Ma said, winking at me as I got into the front passenger's seat after helping Pop into the back. Buttons sat on his lap with her face turned toward the window.

It was dark, but the city of Austin was still awake somehow. Bright lights and traffic.

Pop got to snoring soon after he'd settled in the back. We listened to his rhythmic breathing.

Inhale. Exhale. Inhale. Exhale.

We headed west.

Making Small Talk

"So, how are things going for you, Trudy?" Ma's eyes stared steadily ahead at the miles of road before us.

I must've been trying to wake her up some. "I had my first kiss, Ma," I told her. I couldn't believe I'd told her that.

She nodded her head before she said anything and blinked her eyes several times.

"Who was it?"

"Jerome."

"Do you like him?" she asked. I could see how tight her knobby hands held the steering wheel.

"No, well, I did. It didn't work out anyway, Ma. He moved back to Michigan."

"I'm sorry." Ma nodded her head again. I felt like I was talking to Pop.

"I'm not."

"Some things just aren't meant to be," she told me. "As your body keeps going through the transition from girl to woman, you're going to be even more attracted to boys."

I picked at my nails like Pop picks at his scabs.

"You're going to make choices that will affect your life forever. I pray you'll make the right ones," Ma said.

"Hey, look at the cow! It's peeing!" I pointed at a pretend cow on the side of the road. I scrunched up my eyes tight, feeling incredibly stupid.

I had to change the subject, but a peeing cow?

Ma sighed. She'd been driving for hours. The radio stations were all fuzzy and so was her eyesight. Buttons whined and kept spinning around my lap, unable to get comfortable.

We decided to stop at a hotel. Ma couldn't drive any farther. "We'll have to make up the miles tomorrow," she said, "I'm getting too old to be adventurous." Pop was still snoring. Inhale. Exhale.

Passing Time

We checked into the desert-colored Budget Inn in Sanderson, the only place we could find that didn't require a pet deposit.

We had a hard time waking Pop, and he went right to bed once he got inside the hotel.

Her eagerness fading, Ma lay down for a nap too.

I wandered around the hotel with Buttons on a long leash. She kept snorting because she sniffed up so much dust. Everything seemed so lonely out in the middle of nowhere. The only interesting thing I noticed was ants so big I could've walked them on a leash.

I took out some of my homework and sat on the steps outside our hotel room, almost wishing I was in school. I wasn't quite ready to write Ro-Ro a letter yet.

For dinner, we left Buttons in the room and went to an all-you-can-eat diner. Our bald waiter had sweat beads pooling all over his head. Our food was all the same—greasy.

With sleep still in his eyes, Pop told me, "Eat up, Trudy, it all costs the same."

Not wanting Pop to know that I hated the diner, I grabbed another plate of food to pick at.

"Eat up, it all costs the same." He said it four more times before we left. I saw the greasy bald-headed waiter roll his eyes the last time he filled my glass with water. I looked over at Ma, who looked as concerned as I felt.

What was wrong with my father?

Looking Up in the Sky

After dinner, the three of us decided to take Buttons for a walk. The sun had started to set and colors whirled together with the clouds. Yellow, purple, pink, orange, and blue all dabbed together with a paintbrush.

Pop's dry hand held my left hand and Ma's warm hand squeezed my right hand tightly every once in a while, as if she were saying "I love you." I was right in the middle between the two of them. A good place to be.

I saw the first star and, just like when I was a kid, I made a wish. Star light, star bright . . . first star I see tonight . . . I wished that my family would always be happy.

We walked to the grocery store for some cold sodas. On the walk back, the dark sky was lit with many glowing stars. I never knew there were so many. Or that they could be so bright.

Ma pointed to a hazy patch in the sky, "I think that's the Milky Way."

Pop nodded and squeezed my hand. He always had a way of speaking without words.

"Dew Drops" and the Wonderful Earth

As I woke up, I was surprised that I felt like staying in the hotel bed longer, even though the sheets were scratchy and smelled like paint.

Ma put an old cassette tape in the stereo after we'd been on the road for hours. I shifted in my chair because my legs were feeling numb.

We all sang along to Ma's favorite song, "Dew Drops." I don't know the exact words, but it goes something like, "Take a look around . . . dew drops glisten on the ground, take a look at life . . . there is so much more to be found . . ."

"Maybe driving all this way was a bad idea," Ma said when she pulled off to the side of the road to stretch. Buttons jumped out, and when I walked her my legs went from numb to stiff. Pop didn't get out of the car.

"It's a fine idea," I told her. I felt thankful that our gas tank was full, for there was nothing around but nature everywhere.

Finally, I could see a haze of mountains in the distance, and happiness warmed my heart that Ma was going to see the park, even if we were exhausted.

A roadrunner zipped across the road and disappeared before I could blink. That seemed like a good sign to me. It wasn't fake like the cow I'd pretended to see. It wasn't peeing, either.

We saw three more roadrunners and so many different kinds of plants. One cactus looked like a giant candleholder with blooming flowers in each of its hands.

We piled back into the car with a sigh.

"Hey, what is that?" Ma pointed from the driver's seat after we drove through Study Butte. I knew better than to follow the crooked bend of her finger. Instead, I tried to make out what the figure in the distance was.

"Is it a dog?" Pop guessed. When we got closer, Ma parked the car and we saw that it was a coyote. Buttons, her hackles raised, started growling, a low, deep protective growl.

"Easy, girl," I whispered.

The coyote, with its triangular face and black-tipped tail, stopped and stared at us. We stared right back for about ten minutes before it turned and trotted away.

Ma drove us through the most majestic mountains. I never thought that mountains would be as special as running into a coyote, but they were.

My neck hurt from trying to look in every direction. The land was like the Sonora sky—yellow, purple, pink, orange, and blue all run together. I didn't even miss the color green.

Our old station wagon made it up steep mountains and down deep valleys. I saw that Ma had goosebumps as she hummed, "mmmhmmm . . . take a look at life . . . there is so much more to be found . . ."

A Mountain and a Funeral

When we got to Alpine, we all grew quiet. I don't know if it was from seeing so many sights at Big Bend or from realizing what brought us out there in the first place.

As soon as we'd checked into the hotel, Ma called Aunt Robyn to let her know we'd made it. She got the directions she needed and scribbled them on a notepad. "Again, Robyn," I heard Ma whisper into the phone, "I'm so sorry about Frank." We went to the funeral service at the First United Methodist Church of Alpine, while Buttons seemed happy to stay at the hotel. The church looked old and so did Aunt Robyn. She probably thought the same thing about my parents. Aunt Robyn gave me a strong hug. All during the service the only thing I could focus on was the heavy scent of her perfume.

After the funeral, we went to Aunt Robyn's for a family gathering. The house was far away from downtown, but Alpine is so small we were there in ten minutes.

Pop inspected a cactus on the porch. "It's an ocotillo," Aunt Robyn said as she opened her door for us.

I ate tortilla bites with cream cheese in the middle and listened to the adults talk about what a nice person Frank DeLong had been. Pop only nodded his head.

Aunt Robyn was an art professor at Sul Ross. I admired all the ceramic bowls she had in her house. Some were filled with little treats that people were picking at. She also had photographs everywhere.

One old photo caught my eye. Uncle Frank and Pop were dressed as little soldiers and had plastic guns strapped over their shoulders. I couldn't imagine my father ever being that young.

I left the house and headed toward a mountain, only a short walk away. Up, up, and up I climbed until the town looked even smaller.

I could make out the neat rows of houses and could see the candy red university up on a mountain at the opposite end of Alpine.

I sat on a rock and took in such deep breaths of dry air that my lungs both tickled and ached. I sat up there just looking for more than an hour before I wrote Ro-Ro her letter.

A Turkey and a Tornado

Austin seemed a little different to me after our trip to the desert. Too many cars and not enough air. But I soon got back into the groove and managed to catch up on schoolwork before Thanksgiving break.

On Thanksgiving, Ma and I set the table and gathered the fixings while Pop napped. He woke up with a jolt when there was a crack of thunder overhead.

We turned on the TV and heard the weather forecast: over a 90 percent chance of thunderstorms. It started to rain, rain, rain. And rain some more. Buttons kept scratching at the door to go outside, but then wasn't brave enough to go out alone. I put on an old pair of sandals and grabbed an umbrella to walk her outside. It was afternoon, but it looked like midnight.

A red warning strip kept blinking at the bottom of the TV screen. A reporter announced that a tornado had touched down in Buda, about twenty miles to the south of us, and tornadoes were moving north near I-35 toward Austin.

"Take cover in the center of the house with as many walls surrounding you as possible," the reporter instructed.

None of us moved. We kept watching the news and looking outside. Fifteen minutes later, the winds were ripping through south Austin and the rain was blowing sideways. Buttons began howling.

On the radar, the reporter pointed out a cell that was headed toward the airport. Right in the path was Dutch Avenue.

We ran to the pantry and huddled together near the soda cans and rolls of paper towel. Ma held Buttons tightly in her arms, but she couldn't stop her from shaking.

"What's going on?" Pop asked. His eyes were looking toward his greenhouse.

"Just a storm, dear," Ma said in her brave voice.

The wind started roaring and we could hear something rip off the side of the house.

The terrible winds were over quickly, but the rain continued. When it finally let up, we looked at the damage outside and at the river rushing through the ditch. A few shingles had blown off the roof and the rain gutter was gone, but Pop's greenhouse still stood.

"This isn't quite the cleanup this house needs," Ma said. "How can I keep up with it all?"

When it came time for dinner, we counted our blessings. I know that turkey tasted different, and not just because Pop hadn't cooked it this Thanksgiving.

Ro-Ro's Happiness Shines

In early December, Ro-Ro's stepdad came back home.

"For good?" I asked her.

"Nothing is ever for good if you think about it," Ro-Ro replied.

"Well, you know what I mean."

"They seem happier than ever, so I guess that's a good sign. Mama's belly is starting to get so big and she seems like she's glowing."

Another good sign for Ro-Ro was Mr. Yardley taking her aside to talk about her "mathematical capabilities."

"Rhonda," he said, "I think you have what it takes to be in the honors class next semester. Are you willing to give it a go?" Mr. Yardley patted her on the shoulder.

Ro-Ro said she beamed when she replied, "I, Roshanda, know what I am capable of."

"I bet you intimidated him," I said.

"I hope so," she said with a laugh.

And then, as an early Christmas present, Kenneth

gave her a shiny silver ring with a tiny heart engraved in the middle.

I hate to say it, but I felt jealous of how that ring shone on her hand.

Cereal Boxes, a Can of Veggies, and Underwear

When the toilet paper roll ran low, I went into the bathroom cupboard to get a new one. I found two full boxes of cereal and a can of mixed vegetables sitting calmly next to the bathroom supplies.

I had to laugh, because we always keep food in the kitchen pantry.

"Hey, Ma, when did you start putting food in the bathroom?" I asked. I held out the box of frosted cornflakes in my hand. Ma gave me a funny look.

"Did you do that?"

"Ma, then why would I be asking about it?"

"Sorry," she said. "I'm so exhausted these days I can't keep track of everything. I'm sure it was Pop. He's been misplacing things around the house lately. He took off his wedding ring and put it at the back of the sock drawer last week. I thought we'd never find it."

During dinner the following week, Pop announced, "I need to buy some underwear."

"But honey, you have a drawer full of underwear," Ma said.

"I don't have any," Pop argued. Ma quit slicing her pork chop and left the kitchen table. She looked in his underwear drawer and sure enough—no underwear.

Dinner was put aside and the hunt for the white briefs began. We looked in the washing machine, in the dryer, in the bathroom. Ma ended up finding the underwear pile at the back of Pop's side of the closet near his shoes.

"How did they get there?" Ma asked, a stressed-out look on her face. She dug her nails into her hair, scratching at the roots.

Pop and I both shrugged our shoulders at the same time.

"We just might have to get a surveillance camera for this house," Ma tried to joke. When we came back into the kitchen, we found Buttons on the kitchen table helping herself to our pork chops.

"It's official," Ma said, "we definitely need surveillance cameras for this house."

Old Timers

Singing Christmas carols, we decorated our house and put up the fake Christmas tree. Pop couldn't remember the words to the songs, but he hummed along.

Some days were warm and some days were cold. Pop didn't go outside on any of those days, so I watered his pansies and trimmed some of the brown branches off his miniroses.

Ma wrapped Christmas presents and put them underneath the tree. But, like Pop's underwear, they too disappeared.

We found the packages stacked behind the couch.

Ma didn't have to ask me how they got there. We knew it was Pop's doing.

He wasn't losing only things. He had a hard time remembering words, too. The car was sometimes a car and sometimes a train. Pop referred to most birds as ducks. And I was Laura Bell most of the time. Ma didn't even act surprised the first time she heard him call me that.

Instead of going outside to take care of his plants, Pop gazed through the window at his greenhouse. Ma and I started mowing the yard and clipping the shrubs.

When I called home to get picked up after school one day, Ma wasn't there. Pop got all tongue-tied trying to explain, "She . . . she's . . . she's at the place." His next sentence was all babble.

That day, Ma and I had a talk about the changes in Pop. I think we'd been avoiding it for a long time. Talking about it made it even more real—like a serious problem.

Ma made an appointment with our doctor to find out what was going on.

Dr. Modge asked Pop the names of the days of the week, who was president, and other questions that people can usually answer easily. He also had him do simple things like touch his nose with his finger.

Pop must not have done so well. The doctor diagnosed Pop with dementia.

"Dr. Modge thinks it might be Alzheimer's," Ma told me. Before that, I thought the disease was really called Old Timers.

The Long Walk

"What made Pop sick?" I asked Ma. I kept thinking about what the doctor said over and over again. I couldn't concentrate on anything else.

I was so worried about Pop I could hardly look at him. I didn't want to watch him slipping away.

"I don't know," Ma said. She sat with her hands clasped together tightly. The veins in her hands looked like a complicated maze.

After she finished her sentence, I could feel my stomach tense up. How could my mother not know? How could there be no answers?

"I'm going for a walk," I told Ma.

As soon as I said, "Walk," Buttons cocked her head, then torpedoed for her leash. "Fine, girl," I whispered. My fingers pinched the hook of the leash onto her collar. "Fine."

Ma sighed one long breathy sigh, but it seemed as if she understood. I had to get away—from her, from Pop, from the disease.

I walked. I took the path Pop and I used to take.
Button's toenails tapped on the concrete while my feet
shuffled.

I saw flowers growing that Pop might've known the
name for. I thought of all the questions without answers.
How did it happen? Why was it happening? What was
going to happen? Shuffle and tap, we kept walking.

I walked so far the bottoms of my feet burned and
my calves ached. Buttons hunkered down and refused
to walk any more. "C'mon, girl, don't give up on me,"
I told her. She wouldn't budge.

I picked her solid body up in my arms. She heaved
from panting so hard. I kissed her on the top of her
head and carried her on that long journey home. I
couldn't give up on Pop either.

Talking to Ms. Gwen

Ms. Gwen passed back our assignment. My paper was marked with a B and a note that said, "Come see me after school."

The grade didn't bother me as much as Ms. Gwen's note. My fingers scratched at the red ink. I kept thinking of how I'd disappointed her.

"I'm concerned about you, Trudy," she told me after the last person walked out of her classroom.

"I meant to do more research," I interrupted. I looked down at my bag and zipped a zipper. "I'll work harder on the next project."

"It isn't that," Ms. Gwen said. "I know you can write something stronger than that. It just seems like you're . . . unhappy."

I looked up at Ms. Gwen's eyes and knew she'd be able to tell if I was lying. "Pop's not well," I told her.

"Hopefully, he'll be getting better soon," she said. Her voice sounded as cheery as her eyes looked.

"He's got Alzheimer's or some kind of dementia. There's no way to be sure." I had to look away from her eyes. "There's nothing anyone can do about it. He's having a hard time right now."

"You must be too," Ms. Gwen said. She gave me a hug and though I tried hard not to, I cried.

"My mother is in a nursing home," Ms. Gwen told me, after passing me a tissue. "She's diabetic and after she broke her hip, I knew I couldn't take care of her like she needed. It's hard to watch someone you love so much suffer."

"Does she remember you when you see her?" I asked.

"Yes, Trudy, she does. I think it would be hard if she didn't. Not everyone where she lives remembers who they are, though. I feel sad visiting her sometimes."

"That's what I'm afraid of the most. Not feeling sad, really, but that Pop won't remember who I am."

"It'll be one of the toughest parts to deal with, but you have to know you were and are loved. You have to find a special way of remembering him, especially when he starts to get worse," she told me. "You have to keep looking ahead at the future while still reminding yourself of special things from the past."

There was silence between us for a moment. In that moment I felt relief and comfort.

"I'm here anytime you need to talk," Ms. Gwen told me.

"Thank you."

The Live Oak

The ride in the car with Ma was quiet, like it must've been with Pop and Buttons at home. I thought of Ms. Gwen's voice encouraging me to find a way to remember Pop. When I told Ma my idea, she said it would be a thoughtful surprise.

We decided to start looking. Hardly any cars were parked at the plant nursery. Our on and off again rain showers were probably keeping people away.

"What kind of tree are you thinking of?" Ma asked as we walked down rows of different shades of green.

"I don't know," I answered.

When someone from the nursery asked if we needed help, I told her I was looking for something that would take root easily. "It has to be hearty," I said.

The woman showed me Bradford pears, crepe myrtles, and Arizona ash trees. Ma and I inspected each one carefully. They weren't what I was looking for.

"What about this one?" I asked as I studied a tree with dark, glossy leaves. Some of the newer leaves were a brighter green. The base of the tree was more like a branch than a trunk, but there was something about it that spoke to me.

"It's a live oak," the woman explained. "They're great shade trees, but they can grow to be quite massive. They don't lose their leaves like other trees."

"It's the one," I told Ma. It wasn't a flowering tree like the green hawthorn, but it would have presence. It would be full of life year-round, a tree that would be there long after we were gone.

Ma agreed, and after we'd bought the tree and a few other supplies, we folded down the backseat and loaded it up for the ride home.

We decided the perfect spot would be adjacent to my tree. Digging a hole for the live oak was more challenging than planting it. Rain started sprinkling on Ma and me as we shoveled dirt.

After hours of work, we finally staked the tree and spread mulch around the base. "I'll go get Pop," I told Ma, as I wiped my dirty hands on my pants.

"I have something to show you outside, Pop," I said as I grabbed his hand and led him out back.

"What's this?" Pop asked when I pointed at the new addition to our backyard.

"A live oak, Pop," I explained, "in honor of you."

Shopping News

Ro-Ro and I went shopping before Christmas, to get out and to catch up on things.

She'd been so busy hanging out with Kenneth and I'd been so busy worrying about Pop.

Walking through the food court, I told Ro-Ro, "My father is sick."

"With what?" she asked.

"Alzheimer's," I told her and explained everything.

Ro-Ro gave me a hug, a warm hug like the one she gave me the day we met. "Are you going to get it someday?" she asked.

"I don't know, Roshanda. The doctors still don't know enough about the disease. They're not even sure what's wrong with him. It's like his brain is going to mush."

"How's your mom taking it?" she asked.

At that moment, I felt awful for not worrying more about Ma. I'd thought only about Poor Pop, and—I hate to admit it—about Poor Me.

"We're all taking it pretty bad. Even Buttons. She's more glued to his side than ever. It's been happening so fast, too. He isn't the same person anymore. His sentences don't always make sense, and he can't even sign his own name."

"What are you going to do?" Ro-Ro asked.

"I guess I just want to help him any way I can," I told her. I could feel my tears close and ready to overflow.

"Mama thinks she might be having another boy," Ro-Ro said. "I'm hoping I have a little sister."

I was so grateful she'd changed the subject. "I think you're so lucky. I wish I had a little brother or sister," I told her.

"And change all those diapers?" Ro-Ro laughed, then leaned over and gave me another hug.

It wasn't quite the same, but I knew I had a sister.

Adding to Our Family

Ma crocheted a baby blanket for Ro-Ro's family for a Christmas present, even though they probably had dozens already. We three stopped by Ro-Ro's house, just a few blocks from ours, to deliver it. Ma also brought some peanut butter fudge she had made.

The fudge hadn't quite set. When I asked if she was sure she wanted to give it to them, I think I hurt Ma's feelings.

Ma and Ro-Ro's mom, Linda, hit it off right away. Linda didn't seem to care that the fudge looked like soup. I regretted saying anything about it to Ma.

Before we left, Ma and Linda seemed like the best of friends. They were laughing and swapping stories about swollen feet and food cravings.

Before long Ma and Linda were calling each other almost as often as Ro-Ro and I did. Ma also offered to babysit once in a while, which I think Ro-Ro appreciated more than anyone.

Pop made several friends that day too. Ro-Ro's stepdad, Derrick, came over and shook his hand. Pop responded with a nod of respect, even though the two didn't say anything to each other.

Pop was especially interested in Miles, Quentin, and John—Ro-Ro's younger brothers. He sat on the floor and watched them all steer a remote control car.

When Miles drove the car right into Pop's foot, Pop laughed his thick laugh. A bell rang in my memory. It had been a long time since I'd heard him laugh like that.

Sitting with those kids on the floor, he looked like one of them.

My father was turning into a child.

Christmas Prayers

Christmas time had a different feel to it. The lights were lit, but I couldn't feel any sparkle inside.

Roshanda was so busy with her family that she and I didn't even have a chance to get together. I sat at home thinking of the Tower laughing with her three brothers. She had her stepfather with her, while my father was slipping away from me.

On Christmas Eve we went to the midnight church service, and I felt warm on that cold night. Red poinsettias, wreaths, and a cross bright with candles made the church feel like home, even though it had been awhile since I'd been there.

When I lit my candle during the singing of "Silent Night," I prayed that Pop would get better, even though I knew Pop might get worse and there was no medicine to help him.

Christmas morning was quiet and presents no longer seemed important. The present I wanted most was to have Pop back like he used to be.

Vienna Attire

Instead of watching TV all night, which is what we usually do on New Year's Eve, Ma bought us tickets to *A Night in Old Vienna* at the Majestic Theater in San Antonio. Buttons went to stay with the Johnsons. Ro-Ro promised me they'd take good care of her.

I had never been to the symphony and neither had Ma or Pop, though Ma had always dreamed about it. The idea was part of her New Year's resolution to make those somedays happen.

I decided to wear a black satin skirt and a blue velvet shirt. Ma dressed up too, only she wore a white blouse with a skirt.

Pop sat on the couch motionless as Ma and I got ready.

"Honey, come on, we have an hour and a half trip to make!" Ma fussed.

"Grace, settle down." Pop hadn't used Ma's first name in a long time. It was almost a shock hearing him say it. Ma has always been "Ma" to me.

Pop got up stiffly and went into the bedroom to change. When he came out, he was wearing white shorts, a shirt with a button-down collar, and a half-tied tie. He had black socks on, but no shoes.

Ma took one look at him and laughed. I had to fight the urge to giggle.

Pop's face got real red. He tried to say something, but he could only make noises—"Jgggmff."

After kissing him on the cheek, Ma took Pop into the bedroom to change.

Pop came out of the room well dressed, but he still had a frown on his face.

A New Year's Eve Nightmare for Someone

Ma tried rushing us into the car. She tried to hustle Pop especially. We were running late, as usual.

Pop was sulking by walking extra slow, I thought, to irritate Ma. She scratched at her scalp and guided him into the front seat.

We hit almost every red light on the way out of Austin. South Interstate 35 was at a standstill and Ma slapped her thigh and growled, "We're not going to make it!"

It was hard to tell who was grumpier, Ma or Pop.

Traffic cleared up, but an impatient motorcyclist weaved between the lanes. If we were going close to seventy, then he was going at least ninety.

Ma shook her head in frustration. "He's going to cause an accident!"

When we got near New Braunfels, traffic backed up again.

Ma exited illegally—the tires went bump on the ground and we dipped down low before we made it to the access road.

We inched along on the side road, but escaped the heaviest part of traffic on the highway.

About ten miles later, we saw the problem. On the highway we saw several police cars, two ambulances, a fire truck, and a flatbed truck towing a battered motorcycle.

"Oh, Lord," Ma muttered in a low voice. So there had been an accident.

None of us said anything as we caught a glimpse of the motorcyclist on a stretcher. He was being rushed into one of the ambulances.

I watched the lights spin around like propellers and listened to the blare of sirens as the ambulance weaved through traffic on its way to the hospital. We were quiet for the rest of the drive to San Antonio.

Things Lighten Up

We made it to San Antonio a couple of hours before the concert began.

"What the heck." Ma smiled, not so grumpy. Seeing the accident changed us in some way, at least it changed Ma and me. "What do ya'll think about staying downtown?" she asked. "Let's make the most of it."

We drove around downtown San Antonio checking the rates at a few hotels. Most of them were either booked or charged over $200.

We went to the Menger Hotel, a place that felt a little too expensive. Ma just said, "Let's give it a try." Pop followed along after giving Ma a nod.

A young manager wearing a silver tie helped us. "What can I do for you folks?" he asked as he looked all three of us over.

When Ma asked about available rooms, he told us the prices.

"We're going to have to pass," she said. I felt disappointed that Ma wasn't making the most of it, even though she was trying.

"Wait, we do have a cancellation on a suite," the manager said as we started to walk away.

"A suite? But how much?" Ma asked.

"I can get you a deal for ninety dollars."

"What the heck," Ma said again. Pop simply nodded. Again.

The hotel was fantastic—ancient wallpaper and history all over.

We took our credit-card-style key and opened the room to our suite. "Our suite," I kept saying it just because I like the word suite. The Teddy Roosevelt Suite.

There was a huge kitchen, a dining area, and the fanciest bathroom with a spa-style bathtub.

Pop and I explored the room, which was almost the size of our house. I couldn't help it—I jumped on my bed.

The manager sent up some bathroom supplies and complimentary tickets for breakfast in the morning.

The Performance

The Majestic Theater didn't seem like much on the outside. Mostly just an entrance on a strip of old connected buildings.

It was like a human zoo watching all the people walking through the doors. One woman had emeralds and diamonds around her neck and a fur coat draped over her shoulders. A woman standing near her was wearing a jeans dress.

We walked up the stairs to our section. The stage and the architecture were amazing—kind of Arabian, kind of Spanish. Lights, stars, and moving clouds illuminated the painted globe ceiling. Pop looked up at it with an amazed look on his face.

All of the instruments hummed together, a signal that the performance was about to start. I could feel goosebumps rising on my skin in anticipation of my first symphony experience. High above the stage in the mezzanine section, I felt drawn to everything below me.

I looked over at Ma and her eyes were wide and dreamy. She had a happy, peaceful look on her face, a look I hadn't seen for too long.

Even in the dimly lit theater, Pop managed to stay awake.

"So, Trudy, what did you think of the experience?" Ma asked when it was over. We each held on to one of Pop's arms and steered him through the people zoo.

"Amazing," I told her. "What about you, Pop? What did you think of the theater?"

"What theater?"

Ma and I just ignored him, as mean as that sounds.

Fireworks Full of Hope

After relaxing for a few hours in the luxury of our hotel—our suite—we followed the crowds down to San Antonio's Riverwalk.

Lights draped on the trees made the area feel like a colored, twinkling fantasy. I felt the twinkle on the inside too.

I could see my breath cutting through the cold air.

Pop placed his hands over his red nose and coughed a long cough. Ma wrapped her arm around him and held him close to her.

We stopped at a small shop where each of us got a greedy large cup of hot chocolate and a doughnut. I chose a chocolate-covered doughnut with sprinkles on it. I felt a little sick to my stomach after eating it, but I didn't want to complain.

In some places, we had to walk around the watery maze single file because of the large crowds. Ma never took her eyes off of us, Pop especially.

Midnight grew near. New hopes. New dreams. New memories.

All of us gathered along the Riverwalk stood still and shouted out the countdown:

"10 . . .9 . . .8 . . .7 . . .6 . . .5 . . .4 . . .3 . . . 2 . . .1 . . . happy new year!"

A burst of fireworks shot up in the sky. Bursts of glitter filled my heart with thoughts of a happy new year.

An Unfortunate Break, but Not So Bad

Ro-Ro came over to spend the night before Christmas break was over. Ma gave us the choice of roller-skating or going to a movie.

"A little exercise might be fun for you," Ma said, poking herself in the stomach. "I should go with you girls."

"Why don't you come?" I asked.

"No," Ma said. "I'm too old. You young girls go without me."

At the skating rink, I laced up the stiff boots with wheels on them. Holding hands, Ro-Ro and I glided out on the glossy wooden floor.

I felt clumsy, like when I tried dancing, only I had eight small wheels attached to my feet.

Ro-Ro got the hang of it fast. We separated, and she started taking the curves with a speedy attitude.

I tried to keep up with her, not wanting to admit that I probably couldn't.

When a song full of beat and excitement came on, I decided to speed my slow feet up to match the song and Ro-Ro. My feet felt like they were shuffling like Pop's.

I took the corner almost as fast as Ro-Ro did, but I tripped over my own foot and down I went.

I stretched my left hand out to break my fall. I broke my wrist instead, but not bad.

I tried not to cry as I raced off the rink so I wouldn't make a scene, at least not anymore than I already had.

The pain was more in my stomach than in my wrist. I felt shaky.

Ro-Ro called Ma. Only when I started talking to Ma did I get teary-eyed.

I held my wrist with my right hand. And, with Ro-Ro's branches around me, we waited on the curb outside the rink for Ma to pick us up.

A Movie Instead

Even though Ma picked us up as fast as she could, a thousand cars seemed to pass by the rink before she got there.

Numbness had crept in and my fingers tingled a bit. They were really swelling up, too.

"Trudy, do you think you need to go to the emergency room?" Ma asked.

I thought about how much it had cost Ma the time she had to take me in for chest pains. It ended up being nothing serious, but it still cost a fortune. I responded to her question with a no.

By the time we got back to my house, I could wiggle my wrist a little bit. Ma decided to make an appointment as early as possible the next day. After taking some pain medication, I didn't mind waiting till morning either.

"Are you sure you still want to spend the night?" I asked Ro-Ro.

She nodded her head yes and helped wrap a white bandage around my wrist. Ma placed a frozen sponge in a tightly sealed plastic bag over it.

Ma rented us a movie, too, to keep my mind occupied. I rested my arm on an old stuffed E.T. doll. My wrist fit right in the crook of his alien neck.

I was awake much of the night, groggy from the pills, but not able to talk like I would at a normal sleepover. Pain shot up my arm and into my elbow. Lying on my stomach wasn't an option, and I had to be careful whenever I changed position.

What luck.

Wrapping It Up

Ma took me to the doctor's office the next morning.

"So what happened, Trudy?" Dr. Modge questioned. He wrote on a pad my story of me falling down. I didn't mention the embarrassing thud I'd made when I hit the rink.

He felt my wrist and hand all over, while I tried not to complain about how he was hurting me. He poked my fingers with the tip of a pin.

"Can you feel that?" he wanted to know.

"Of course."

Dr. Modge ordered X-rays and the technician had me place my arm in at least five awkward positions.

We waited for them to be processed. Dr. Modge then ordered more X-rays because things looked "inconclusive," as he put it.

After another twenty minutes of turning my arm this way and that, all the X-rays were finally taken and Dr. Modge had another look.

The verdict? A hairline fracture.

I felt ashamed that it wasn't something more serious.

A technician came to make a splint for my arm—half bandage, half cast. His small hands smoothed the cast material over the bends of my forearm.

"Your granddaughter is a brave one," he said to Ma.

Ma's face flushed with color, but she didn't correct him. Instead she scratched at the roots of her hair. I wasn't brave enough to say anything either.

'Twas the Night Before School Started Again

I had a hard time sleeping that night before school started again. I wanted a longer break. I wanted more time to spend with Ro-Ro, more time to spend gardening with Pop.

Ma and I spent my last afternoon cleaning up all the overgrown vegetation in our yard.

"This is too much," Ma said. "I'm getting too old to be stressed about taking care of these kinds of things."

"No, you're not." Despite my splint I managed to drag loads of trash to the front. Ma rolled her eyes at me.

I made sure to take special care of the plant Pop gave me. A sword-shaped green shoot was starting to push through the dirt.

As it grew dark I had that same ugly feeling of dread, the feeling I'd felt before. I didn't want another school week to begin and the more I thought about it, the sicker I felt.

Ma and Pop were both in bed already and the house was depressingly dark. I thought about waking Ma up for company, but I decided not to. I called out to Buttons, who must have been snoring too loud to hear me. I had to face the dark alone.

The last time I checked my clock it was 1:13 AM.

I felt tired and gloomy the next day, too. I worried about what Ma would do with Pop when she had to run errands. I felt sad that I couldn't spend more time at home.

My splint drew a lot of attention, though. Maybe it wasn't such bad luck.

Even Ashley, Miss High and Mighty, asked me what happened.

I looked her in the eye and said, "I wrestled a grizzly bear." Then I walked away, trying to hold back a laugh. Lying wasn't my greatest gift.

The Things Pop Says

I don't think I've ever heard Pop say one bad thing about anyone.

He'd always had a kind way of putting the truth into perspective. Or at least keeping his comments to himself.

But that sure changed.

Pop started saying anything that came to him. Good or bad. Mostly, you could hardly understand him, but in some cases he unfortunately made sense.

Ma, Pop, and I were at a department store getting me a new long sleeve shirt plus a few other odds and ends—toothpaste, shampoo, tape, and a package of socks for Pop.

We were also looking at a few things we didn't need. Like candy.

We walked down the candy aisle looking at all the choices—many kinds of chocolate, gummy worms, cinnamon imperials. Ma grabbed a bag of miniature candy bars. Just as she tossed it into the cart, Pop blurted out, "You . . . you need all those?" He poked at the meat on his stomach.

"He doesn't mean that," I whispered to Ma.

"He probably does," she snapped. "Who knows with him anymore."

Cartoons and the Ring

Mr. Yardley gave us a math project that was surprisingly fun. We had to find a cartoon and draw a grid over it. Then we had to draw the cartoon on a larger scale using the grid.

Even though Ro-Ro was now in honors and had more requirements to meet, she still had some of the same assignments I had. We decided to work on our cartoon projects together.

Ro-Ro's mom greeted me at the door. "Want a drink, Sweetie?" she asked. Linda's belly was starting to get large and her ankles were swollen with water.

"The doctor told you to stay off your feet," Ro-Ro fussed.

Miles came over and sat in my lap while we were copying lines, trying to make our drawings look exactly like the cartoons. Miles felt warm and solid on my legs. His hair smelled like peanuts.

When there was a knock at the door, Ro-Ro got up

to answer it. It was Kenneth. I could tell by the way he was standing that he didn't have good news.

I kept working on my project, but I overheard Kenneth say, "Can we talk outside?"

Ro-Ro looked over at her mother for permission and then looked at me. I looked down immediately. "Fine," Linda said.

Ro-Ro was still outside when I finished my drawing, close to an hour later. I called Ma to pick me up and went out front to tell my friend I was going home.

The Tower was sitting on her front steps crying. Kenneth was nowhere in sight.

"What happened?" I knelt on the step in front of Ro-Ro.

"He said he doesn't think things are working. Then he said I could keep the ring, but I don't want it." She'd taken off the ring with the engraved heart but she had her hand clasped tight around it.

Seeing all those tears made me feel less jealous of the ring.

"I guess we'll have more time to spend together now," I said.

Roshanda tried to smile, but I think my joke made more tears spill out.

Sleet, the Consolation Prize

January was cold, much colder than December. But, like every other winter of my life, it hadn't snowed in Austin.

Three weeks into the new year, there was a slight chance we'd have snow. I watched all the weather reports and looked outside every five minutes. Ma and I wrapped up some of Pop's plants in sheets so they wouldn't freeze. Most of his plants were already brown, though, and weeds grew where there never used to be any.

The clouds did begin to precipitate. By evening, our cold, heavy rainfall had turned to sleet.

Small ice pellets fell to the ground. I'd imagined that sleet would be like hail, but it wasn't. After bundling me up and lecturing me about pneumonia, Ma let me go outside with Pop. I could hardly move with so many layers of clothes on. Buttons had sensibly stayed inside.

Outside, the sleet made tiny taps on my jacket. It wasn't long before I'd had enough of it. My fingers felt raw out in the bitter cold and my skin, red and chapped, began to burn. Then I noticed that Pop had started walking off down the street.

"Where are you going?" I asked him. He looked like a lost tourist.

"Home," he said. I pointed in the other direction. "You just came out, what's the big hurry?" He just kept walking away from me.

"Are you looking for our house?" I called.

"Home," he said. I ran after him, grabbed him by the hand, and led him back to our house.

Ma had hot chocolate waiting for us when we got back inside. I didn't tell her what had happened.

The three of us sat, taking warm sips of cocoa and staring at the sleet.

Iced Over

When I got up to use the bathroom in the middle of the night, I peeked out the window, still holding on to the idea of snow.

No white flakes were falling, but there was an icicle hanging from the ledge above my window. I went to the back porch for a better view. I could see several icicles hanging from the patio cover.

Glistening and holding on for their lives, they looked sharp and dangerous. I sleepily wondered about the chance of an icicle falling at the same time someone was standing directly underneath it.

I shook my head at that thought. It was then that I noticed the green hawthorn's branches were so weighted down with ice that the lowest ones embraced the ground, as if they were bent over in prayer. I wondered if they were praying that the tree might survive through the night. Pop's tree looked so fragile out in the cold, but it wasn't nearly as covered in ice.

I said my own prayer and headed back to bed. I crawled back under the sheets, trying to find the warm spot I'd left. But it was gone. I scrunched up in a tight ball, trying to make a new one.

Glad the Roads Were Bad

I woke up a few hours later to the screaming of my alarm clock.

Ma was in the living room, the remote control in her hand, flipping channels. She soon found a news station. The newscaster looked serious despite the fake looking wig on his head.

"It's a mess out there, Trudy," Ma said, in her gravelly morning voice.

"I know, isn't it amazing?" I told Ma about all the icicles I'd seen and about the branches.

We watched footage showing road conditions. In some places, the ice was two inches thick.

After a few commercials, the newscaster announced, "Due to the winter storm conditions, the following schools have cancelled classes . . ."

Benavidez Middle School was one of the schools listed!

After scarfing down a banana that Ma insisted I eat,

I went straight back to bed. I didn't even brush my teeth. All I wanted was to go back to sleep.

I didn't even care that there was no warm spot in my bed.

A Land Mine Story with Cereal

When I got up, Ma was crocheting in the den while she watched a soap opera. Her knuckles looked like grapes under her skin.

"Are you hungry, Trudy?" she asked. Her eyes watched the television while her hands kept hooking and knotting.

"Don't worry, Ma, just relax. I'll get something for myself."

Pop was sitting at the kitchen table. He was reading the business section of the newspaper. Only it was upside down.

"Morning, Pop."

He nodded.

I grabbed a box of cereal and picked at some of the dry wheat chunks. The cereal was thick in my throat as I swallowed.

"What are you reading?" I asked him.

"About the war."

I could see stock market numbers on the page facing me. I wasn't sure how to respond.

"What's the latest news?"

"They rescued the boys."

I didn't say anything. I just waited for Pop to continue. I could understand his words, but they didn't make sense.

"I was hurt, Laura Bell, but I had to wait for hours. They . . . they . . . res . . . came and got the ones hurt most. I lay in the thing and couldn't move. I couldn't move. I had to go. When they . . . they . . . the people . . . came back for me, my stomach was huge. I couldn't see my feet."

Pop was talking about the land mine. His mind was in France.

He'd never talked to me about the war before.

He went back to reading, the newspaper still upside down.

I tried to picture Pop lying on the ground. In pain, bleeding, and with a swollen bladder.

It's a part of Pop that I can never fully imagine.

A Dinner Date

By late afternoon, the sun came out and the ice began
to melt.

Drip . . . Drip . . . Drip. I watched from my bedroom as it all began to disappear.

The phone rang and Ma immediately called out:
"Trudy, come here!"

As I ran into the living room, I wasn't sure I wanted
to hear what Ma needed to tell me.

"Guess what?" she asked, though it wasn't really a
question. "Linda had the baby! It's a girl!" she shouted.
"She's close to eight weeks early, but she's healthy and
beautiful. They named her Angel."

I thought about what an amazing name that was—
Angel. Somehow, Gertrude doesn't have the same ring to it.

"When can we see her?" I asked.

Pop, aware of all the commotion, got up from his
chair. His eyes seemed to ask, "See who?"

"Soon," Ma said and began humming her song. "We

should cook a special dinner tonight and take some over to the Johnsons," she said.

"But this should be a happy occasion," I teased.

Ma laughed.

We decided to make chicken spinach manicotti, the dish Pop most liked to cook. As we drove to the grocery store to pick up a few things, we were glad the roads had cleared up. We were even more glad that Angel had arrived safely.

All Pitching In

As soon as we got home Ma began scurrying around the kitchen taking out pots and pans.

"We better follow Pop's recipe exactly," I told her, "especially since we're going to be doubling it." She was too excited to be offended.

Ma started boiling the water in an old stockpot that had been her mother's. I dropped the shells in. One of them was shattered.

Ma prepared the chicken, spinach, and cheese stuffing while she directed me in making the sauce.

"Should we use more oregano?" Ma asked. Wanting to please her, I dropped in another pinch.

When it came time to stuff the shells Pop joined us.

Each time Pop tried to fill a shell, his chicken mixture went in one end of the hollow pasta and right out the other. His face was practically purple with frustration after three unsuccessful attempts.

He finally got the hang of stuffing the shells when I

showed him how to hold his hand over one end. I thought about how easily Pop used to do such things.

When the sauce had simmered long enough, Ma held the pan while I ladled the sauce over the stuffed pasta.

Ma put the dish in the oven, and Pop picked at scraps on the table.

The baking manicotti filled the house with wonderful Italian smells that I hoped weren't lying about how our dinner was going to taste.

Taking my first bite, I was relieved to find the smells had told the truth. Our manicotti didn't taste exactly like Pop's, but it was good.

"Glad we stuck to the recipe," Ma said with a wink.

Angel

We dropped off the dinner and a few other things at Ro-Ro's. Pop refused to get out of the car, so Ma just rolled the windows up and locked the doors.

Ro-Ro was so excited that she rushed out as soon as I got out of the car. She practically knocked me over.

"I'm so glad she's a girl!" she yelled.

Ma rushed over and gave her a hug. "Congratulations!" Ma said with so much excitement that you'd have thought it was Ro-Ro's baby.

"You're a big sister," I told her, but then realized how silly that sounded. She'd been a big sister quite awhile. Ro-Ro didn't seem to mind my comment.

"Aunt Rose is here now, but when my stepdad gets back, I'm going to see Angel." Ro-Ro's hands were shaking.

"I was so scared, Trudy," she told me. "Mom started feeling so sick and every time I asked her if she needed anything, she would moan. Then she started to bleed and got real quiet. My stepdad had to rush her to the hospital, but everything is fine," she said. "Fine, fine, fine!"

When she clapped her hands together, I noticed that she wasn't wearing Kenneth's ring anymore.

The Tower stood tall—tall, proud, and happy.

New Hopes, Old Dreams

As soon as the baby came home from the hospital, Ma and I went over to meet her.

Pop went with us but said he was fine staying in the car.

"You don't want to be rude, do you?" Ma asked him. Pop didn't answer. He stared out the window as though he was seeing something from yesterday there.

Ro-Ro invited us in and Ma gave Linda a box of chocolates. "I'm glad she's home now," Ma said.

Both Ro-Ro and her mom replied at the same time, "Me too."

Miles and the other boys hovered above the baby like she was the most precious thing they'd ever seen. She really was precious. Angel. A name as beautiful as the baby.

Linda scooped the tiny baby up and placed her in Ma's arms.

Ma pressed Angel gently against her chest. Her gnarled hands held the baby so tenderly.

"You used to be this big," she said, looking at me. "Actually, this small." Ma slipped her finger into Angel's hand.

"Ready to hold her?" Ma asked. Ro-Ro handed me a baby blanket.

I wasn't sure I wanted to. I'd never held a baby before, and Angel seemed so fragile. But Ma placed her in my lap.

Angel squirmed and produced a sort of grunt that sounded like the noise Buttons makes when she stretches. Angel's tiny body felt so warm and so full of life. When I looked over at Ma, she had tears in her eyes. They started to flow steadily and she began to bawl.

Linda picked Angel up from my lap.

I rushed over to Ma. "Are you OK?"

"I'm fine, but I need to get going. I've got errands to run," Ma said, trying to mask how choked up she still was.

We said quick good-byes and I heard Ma tell Linda how embarrassed she was. "Don't worry about it," she told Ma.

"What happened?" I asked when we got out to the car. Pop was still staring out the window. I shouldn't have said anything. She started crying all over again.

"I'll never meet your children," she told me. "I'm not going to be a part of your most important some-days."

"That's not true," I told her.

"I wish it wasn't. My life is closer to the ending and yours is closer to the beginning."

"Don't say that, Ma," I begged her.

Flushing Out

I heard the sound of water running before I saw the pool of water forming on the hallway carpet. Buttons immediately jumped up to high ground.

"Shut the water off!" Ma yelled as she ran to find out what happened.

"How?" I yelled back.

Ma screamed something and then ran to turn off the water valve.

"This is a nightmare! I've never seen such a mess in my life." Ma reached into the linen closet and pulled out every towel we owned. She tossed a stack to me.

Pop came walking out of the bathroom. His shirt and pants were soaked and his eyes seemed to ask what was happening.

Pop had flushed everything in the bathroom trash can down the toilet and kept on flushing and flushing.

Ma finally shut the valve off, but water sloshed around her feet and all around the floor.

Ma yelled, "Oh my gosh" so many times that I quit counting. Then she started screaming, "I can't handle this!"

"Calm down, Ma." I threw more towels down on the swamp of the carpet.

"Calm down? There's no way. I can't manage this anymore. I can't keep taking care of the house. I can't keep taking care of Pop and you. I can't do it all!" Ma continued yelling until she was blue in the face. She was still yelling when the plumber arrived.

"I think we should sell the house," Ma said after the plumber left, her voice rising to a yell again.

"What are you talking about?"

"Don't get me started!" she warned.

The Last Straw for Ma

Two days after the flood Ma and I were still arguing about selling the house.

I kept my eyes on Ma as she moved from one end of our small kitchen to the other. Back and forth.

"This is it!" Ma wasn't just rubbing her head, she was pulling out strands of hair and tossing them in different directions. "Please don't argue with me."

"But what about school, Ma?" I worried about not seeing Ro-Ro anymore.

"You'll just have to ride the bus if I can't drive you."

"Ma, I don't want to move. I love my room and I love this house. Pop's greenhouse is out there and the trees—we can't leave the trees."

"I can't keep up with it all. Pop can't help anymore and I can't do it all."

"I can help," I offered.

"You already do now, but you have school and . . ."

"Mom, please!"

"It's for the best and it will make life simpler. End of discussion."

No matter what I argued, Ma wouldn't listen.

When I called Ro-Ro, her mom answered. "Please," I pleaded, "you've got to talk some sense into my mother."

"Why? What happened?" Linda asked.

I told her about Ma freaking out and how we were going to have to sell our history.

"I'll see what Derrick and I can do," Linda promised before hanging up the phone. I didn't get to talk to Ro-Ro, but I at least had a chance to vent.

An Offer Declined

I recognized Ro-Ro's family van pulling into our drive-way, but only her stepdad was in it. "Can I speak to your mother?" he asked when I opened the door.

"Sure," I told him, and then ran to get Ma.

"Trudy, where are your manners?" Ma said. "Don't leave guests standing in the doorway."

"Sorry about that," I mumbled.

"Don't worry," Derrick said with a smile. Ma still shot me a look that spelled m–a–n–n–e–r–s, as she pulled her thumb to the side, signaling me to leave the room.

I walked into the kitchen to get a cold glass of water for Derrick, hoping to make up for my rudeness.

As I waited for the water to get cold, I could hear the two of them talking. "Is something wrong, Derrick?" Ma asked.

"Linda told me you were planning on selling this place. I was hoping it wouldn't have to come to that. I'd be happy to help out with the things you need done. I'm not too bad with a hammer and nails, you know."

"I wouldn't inconvenience you like that," Ma said. "You're a wonderful man to offer, but you have a family you need to be thinking of. You can't be worrying about some pitiful old couple."

"I wish you didn't feel that way," he told her. "Just remember that the offer still stands, OK?"

"Thank you, Derrick," Ma said. "But moving will be for the best. We're lucky to know such wonderful people."

Ro-Ro's stepdad was gone before I could give him his glass of water.

Apartment Hunting with Bows and Arrows

The hunt began soon after Ma decided that we were moving. Only we weren't looking at houses, we were trying to find an apartment.

I never knew what a maze Austin was until we started trying to find the right apartment. All I'd ever known was South Austin. All I'd ever known was my neighborhood.

We looked at apartments on all sides of town, big apartments, small apartments, fancy apartments, dirty apartments. After two full days of searching, I felt apartmented out. Ma and Pop seemed to be feeling the same way. Pop was definitely shuffling his legs more than usual.

Soon after we got home on that second day, Ma asked, "What about Village Oaks?" She looked tired and she had bags under her eyes.

"Ma, that place is for senior citizens."

"Your father and I aren't spring chickens, Gertrude."

"What about me and Buttons? A place like that isn't for a kid and a dog."

"While you were at school today, the manager and I spoke—there won't be a problem bringing you or Buttons. I made sure of it."

"But Ma . . ."

"Trudy, I think this is going to be our best option. It's such a nice place." Though Ma was trying to get me to agree with her, she sounded like she'd already made up her mind.

I stormed off to my room. Ma might as well have shot an arrow through my heart.

I imagined how it would be meeting new neighbors. "Hi, my name is Gertrude White. I live in Village Oaks. Yes, that's where all the old farts live."

As I thought about it more, I decided I could introduce myself as Laura. Pop had given me an alias I was proud of. Laura sounds sophisticated, not sticky on the tongue like Gertrude. For the first time, Pop's failing memory caused me to smile.

The Daunting Sign

We planned on moving before the end of the summer, which would certainly ruin my birthday.

Ma talked to a realtor and started working out the details for selling our house. The husky redhead with the large cone-shaped chest helped Ma put our house "on the market."

The For Sale sign was pounded into our front yard.

The spike pierced the earth and my heart too. How could Ma sell our memories?

The sign leaned to the right some, but neither Ma nor I tried to straighten it. Pop didn't care about the sign leaning, but he constantly asked, "What's that thing?"

When Ma or I would tell Pop that we were moving and our house was for sale, his answer was always the same: "Oh."

Anytime you looked out our living room window, you couldn't help but see the large bright orange letters—for sale.

I could see the sign from my bedroom, too. I decided to keep my blinds shut.

I'd lived in the same house for eleven years. I knew the place like the back of my hand. It was home to me. It had always been home to me.

The thought of moving scared me. But it didn't scare me as much as when Pop got sick.

The Waiting Game

When I got home from school that day, nobody was there. Usually, Pop would be taking his nap and Ma would be waiting for me, either at the door or in the driveway. She'd be looking for me as soon as she heard the school bus stop. But the house was locked up.

I unlocked the door, with a sinking feeling in the pit of my stomach.

Ma had left a note:

> Trudy, Pop is not doing so good. Please don't worry, but I have taken him to the emergency room. I love you and will try calling you as soon as I hear something.

I tried not to worry, but that was harder than trying not to blink. I couldn't stop thinking about all the things that could have happened.

An hour later the phone rang. But it wasn't Ma, it was Ro-Ro.

"Ro-Ro," I said so quickly I had to catch my breath, "I can't talk. Pop is in the emergency room. I don't want to tie up the phone line."

"Oh, my gosh," Ro-Ro said, pausing so long I almost hung up on her. "What can I do to help?"

"I have to go," I told her. "Sorry." I hung up the phone, hoping Ma hadn't tried calling.

Another hour went by and Ma still hadn't called. I kept staring out the front window and walking outside on the porch.

Buttons seemed nervous, too, and she kept staring at the front door.

I finally heard a car pull up the driveway. It was Ma. But Pop wasn't with her.

Telling It Like It Is

I was out the front door faster than Ma could get out of the station wagon. I could hear Buttons barking inside the house.

"What happened? Is he OK?"

Ma said nothing at first, but she gave me a hug. My heart felt like it had quit beating. I couldn't tell what kind of news Ma was bringing home with her.

"They admitted him to the hospital. There's fluid in his lungs and his heart is enlarged," she explained. Then she paused, as though she expected me to understand what it all meant.

"But is he OK?"

A single tear crept down the groove in her cheek. Another quickly followed. "Trudy, I don't know."

Ma said nothing else. She walked into the house quickly and went right into the bedroom, closing the door behind her. Buttons scratched at her door to be let in.

I felt hurt. I wanted to shake the information out of her. But I left her alone.

Ma came out of the bedroom not too many minutes later, her nose raw and her eyes looking like she'd glued ladyfingers underneath them.

She gave me another hug and whispered, "I'm sorry," in my ear. "The doctors told me that your daddy has congestive heart failure. They're running all kinds of tests to find out what can be done. He's not doing so good, sweetheart."

I nodded. Like Pop. My own heart felt like it was failing.

Ma grabbed all the things she'd come home for. I scooped Buttons up so we could drop her off at the Johnsons' house on our way to see Pop.

Visiting Pop

We entered St. Paul's Hospital, Ma close to my side.

Walking through the emergency room entrance, I saw at least fourteen exhausted faces look up from their chairs, wondering what our story might be.

I stood straight and forced my face muscles into what must have looked like a smile.

I wanted those faces to see that I was brave. I was brave. Pop was so ill and I was brave.

Ma looked like she was trying to do the same thing, only the dark rings under her eyes said, "Not really." Her yellow-white hair had escaped the tightness of her bun. She'd pulled at it at every stoplight on the way to the hospital.

We said nothing to each other as we walked through icy, bright hallways.

Left. Right. Right.

We stopped near an entrance to a room.

Ma took a deep breath, "This is it."

In my head I repeated, "This is it." That's how I felt inside.

I was brave.

There were six beds, three on either side of the room. Pop was lying in one of them.

My shoulders back and my head high, I walked into the room and saw Pop's name, "White," on a chart before I saw him.

Then I saw his face, though I didn't recognize him. Tubes ran up his nose and an IV stuck out of his arm. I looked down at the chart again to make sure it was my father.

Pop's eyes looked like indentions made by pressing the eraser end of a pencil into a ball of clay. His mouth, which was wide open, looked like an oval carved into that same chunk of swollen clay.

He was sound asleep—a deep, heavy sleep.

I couldn't look at his face anymore. I stared at his hands. His fingers were so thick that each of them looked like an extension of his arm.

His body, large and swollen, was just a breathing lump on the bed. Inhale. Exhale. Seeing his chest rise and fall was the only way I could tell he was alive. Try harder than you have in all your life, I wanted to tell him.

Ma must have seen the look on my face. She must have known I was not brave.

A Time to Remember, or Forget

Ma sat in a reclining chair on Pop's right side and I sat to his left on the edge of his bed.

Glenda, the tall, skinny nurse, brought an extra chair. She scooted it close to me, the metal whining against the floor. She smiled and said, "Make yourself at home."

I couldn't smile back. This was as far away from home as I'd ever been.

I wanted to have Pop asleep in his chair at home, snoring peacefully and comfortably with Buttons lying near his feet.

Pop's head was drawn back and his mouth was open, but there was no soothing snoring. Inside his chest, Pop's lungs rattled like a penny in a tumbling dryer.

Ma rubbed the side of Pop's face like she was trying to wake him up. She whispered, "I love you," in his ear.

I sat in my chair, afraid to look at the other patients and afraid to look at my father. He was still sleeping.

I wanted him to tell me stories I'd never heard. Stories of my grandfather and grandmother, my great-grandparents, too. Stories about what it was like for him growing up. Stories about the war. About his life.

I wanted to be with Pop on one of our walks. I wanted to be picking weeds with him or pruning his plants. Even better, I wanted to be dancing with him in one of our lessons.

A trickle of regret crawled up my spine. I wished I'd enjoyed the dancing lessons more, thought less about my thick feet and more about the warmth of Pop's arms.

Sleeping and Breathing

Pop's oxygen levels began decreasing and one of the machines he was hooked up to started beeping. Glenda came running in. Pop's chest heaved up and down and, for the first time, his eyes opened. Big, scared deer eyes.

Dr. Voigt came down immediately and wrote orders for putting Pop on some kind of ventilation system. I didn't even catch the doctor's first name. I didn't care.

Dr. Voigt looked over at me. He motioned to Ma that he needed to talk to her in private. I left the room, but not without thoughts about trying to listen in.

I went to the vending machines in the waiting room. Neat rows of chip bags didn't entice me. I wasn't hungry. Only hungry to be back near Pop's side.

Ma came and found me. I offered her a sip of the lemon-lime soda I'd chosen, but she shook her head no.

"Dr. Voigt said that your daddy is too unstable to have the surgery he needs right now. His artery is blocked and his sodium levels are too low. We need to pray, Trudy."

And so we did, Ma sitting next to me in the waiting room on a violent orange chair and I sitting in a lemon green one. We held hands and each silently said our own prayer. *I wish I may, I wish I might, have this wish I wish tonight.*

Though Ma's eyes, puffy and dark, looked at me, she was talking to herself, "I should call Linda to pick you up."

"No, Ma, I need to be here." Ma nodded. I needed her and she needed me.

We stayed in the waiting room while the doctors ran more tests and tried to help Pop breathe more easily. When we went back to the room, Pop had a tube running out of his neck.

There was still a rattling in his chest, but he was sleeping again. A deep, heavy sleep.

Wake up, Pop.

I See You

Glenda came back about every thirty minutes to check Pop's vital signs. In the early evening, we heard her loud, concerned "Hmmm." Pop's temperature was 103.4.

Dr. Voigt came and sent Pop to the intensive care unit. There, Pop was assigned his own nurse, who introduced herself as Alice when she met us in the corridor leading to the ICU.

Alice had eyes as intense as Ro-Ro's. Thinking of Ro-Ro for an instant, I wished for a normal moment in my life. Inside, I knew there might not be one for a long time.

Only one person at a time was allowed in to see Pop. Ma encouraged me to visit him first, before the evening visiting hours ended.

I entered the ICU with my shoulders drooping. I felt like the green hawthorn covered in ice. I was not brave.

Alice left the room when I entered.

Seeing Pop in his hospital bed, attached to wires

and on a ventilator, made my knees weak. I knew that I needed to be brave for Pop, even though he was asleep.

I rubbed my hand over his gray, greasy hair.

"Remember that time, Pop, when we went to Alpine?" One tear slid down my cheek. Even if he had been awake, he probably wouldn't have remembered our trip.

"Imagine you're seeing those mountains, Pop. You're down in the valley and you need to climb up that mountain." *Don't let him see you cry.*

I held his hand and sang to him, "Take a look around . . . dew drops glisten on the ground, take a look at life . . . there is so much more to be found . . ."

Don't let him see you cry.

I was still afraid to cry. Crying would make it too real. Ma had cried, though, and I couldn't comfort her. I couldn't comfort Ma.

I closed my eyes and thought of Pop becoming a star in the Milky Way. I was so afraid he was going to die.

Alfred John White

Pop was so close to gone. Gone as in dead. I couldn't stop staring at the medical chart. No, not the medical chart. It was Pop's name. "Alfred John White." Alfred.

I'd never known Pop as Alfred. I'd never thought of him as an Alfred. When I thought of his name, I felt he was more of a person, but a person I didn't know. How much of his life had I missed?

My chest pulled, not because of my past, my scars, but because I was losing Alfred. I'd been losing him for a while.

He meant so much to me, means so much to me. A large part of my past, a smaller part of my present, and a future close to gone.

I felt the same feeling as when I'm afraid to be alone at night. I felt that feeling of fear and emptiness. Ma felt it, too, and we held each other's hands so tight I could feel the bones in her hand cutting off the blood supply in mine.

Ma's tears had stained the makeup on her face. She heaved deep sighs, her eyes looking up to the heavens.

My tears choked me. Instead of flowing out they flowed in and I wanted to throw them up, throw up all my pain.

When Dr. Voigt came in just after midnight, he said Pop's vital signs had improved—his fever was gone and his sodium levels had increased. He told Ma that if she agreed they could do the surgery to unclog his artery. "It won't be without risk, however," he said.

"We have to do what we can," Ma told Dr. Voigt as she signed the forms the hospital required.

They wheeled Pop away to prepare him for surgery. I felt so sick I thought I might pass out. Ma paced back and forth.

We waited four long hours before Dr. Voigt returned. "Your husband is stable," he told Ma. He started explaining specifics about the surgery, but I didn't listen. I kept repeating the word stable over and over.

By late the next day, Pop was out of ICU. He still had a long way to go, but Ma and I felt hopeful.

Home

Everyone from the hospital wanted us to go home. "If there are any changes in Alfred, we'll call first thing," Glenda promised.

Ma and I went home and collapsed. The Johnsons were still watching Buttons for us. I hadn't even talked to Ro-Ro.

I watered the plant Pop gave me and ran my finger along the thick leaves. Blossoms were starting to form— a hint of white showed through the green.

I pressed my head into the pillow, taking in a deep breath of my hair, which I hadn't washed in days. There was something familiar about my own sour smell.

When I woke up hours later, Ma came into my room. I wondered if she smelled my sour scent too. I smelled her light perfume and knew that she was home to me.

"I love you," Ma whispered into my dirty hair.

"I love you too."

Ma and I cleaned up and went back to the hospital.

I thought Pop might be better, might even look like the same old Pop. But he looked the same as when we'd left him.

But the doctors said it was only a matter of time before he was going to come around.

Partial Homecoming

The doorbell rang. "It's Buttons!" I yelled, so excited to have her home. I could hear her barking outside, anxious to get in.

Pushing her way through the door, she practically knocked me over. I picked her up and kissed the top of her button nose. She wiggled in my arms to get down.

Ma knelt down, painful as it must have been for her, and petted her all over. Buttons flipped on her back and kicked out her legs in excitement.

Buttons immediately got up and ran to the bedroom before zipping and zooming into each room. She knew that something wasn't right.

Linda passed Ma a box of canned soups and packaged food. "It isn't manicotti," she said, "but I hope it helps."

"Thank you for your kindness," Ma told Linda and Derrick. "Do you have a second to talk in private?"

I watched as they walked into the kitchen.

"How are you doing, Trudy Booty?" Ro-Ro asked, holding Angel securely in her arms. Angel's eyes were so alert and her fingers were curled into little balls.

"I guess I'm doing all right. She's getting so big," I told my friend as I held the baby's tiny hand in mine.

"She's growing like a weed," Ro-Ro said. Thinking of weeds made me think of Pop. Ro-Ro must've noticed. "I'm so sorry your dad is sick," she told me.

I tried not to cry. "How are things at school?" I asked, quickly changing the subject.

"Good, I guess. Everyone has been asking where you've been. When are you coming back?"

"Soon," I answered.

"I miss you," Ro-Ro said, just as Angel began to wail.

"I miss you too," I told her as I gently rubbed Angel on her back.

Help

"What were you talking about 'in private'?" I asked Ma as soon as the Johnsons left. I couldn't stand not knowing.

"Nothing," Ma said as she lifted a can of chicken soup from the box Linda had brought us. "I'm hungry, aren't you?" She reached for a pot out of the bottom cabinet.

"I can't stand secrets, especially not now," I told her, as I gently took the pot from her hand.

The blood vessels in Ma's face seemed to stand out. "I asked them for help, Gertrude," she admitted. "Pop needs it. I need it," she said, staring at the stove.

"What kind of help?"

"Nothing in particular, at least not right now. But I want to know help is available."

"Ma, I'll do anything I can, too. I can mow the yard and do more housework. I'll cook more," I promised. "Whatever it is, I'll try. I'll help."

"I know you will. When your daddy comes home, he's going to need as much help as possible. I'm thinking about working part-time so we can hire a nurse if we need to. I need your help right now to support any decisions we make."

"Of course," I said, nodding my head in agreement.

We ate our chicken soup before going back to visit Pop at the hospital. Buttons jumped up in Pop's chair at the dinner table as soon as we sat down. She didn't beg. She just curled up into a ball and went to sleep. Neither Ma nor I had the heart to make her get down.

Back to School

Ashley Sanchez was the first person I ran into when Ma dropped me off at school. As she wrapped her arms around me, I saw real human tears in her eyes. She didn't say anything, but her eyes told me what I needed to know. Pop had taught me how to read body language.

I hugged Ashley back, not wanting to hold on to the ugliness between us anymore. I wanted instead to hold on to the friend I once had.

Ro-Ro, protective as ever, walked me to every class that first day. She was so careful with me that she didn't even make any jokes.

Standing at the entrance to his room, Mr. Yardley nodded his head and said, "Welcome, Trudy."

Ms. Gwen's class was the hardest to go to. Ms. Gwen's face was full of concern as she hugged me and said, "Let's hope your father gets better soon."

"It's looking better," I told her. "We're hoping he'll be able to leave the hospital before long."

"How are you holding up?" Ms. Gwen asked.

I felt comfortable enough to tell her I was scared. "I'm not sure what things are going to be like," I said.

"That's how I felt after my mom went into the nursing home. I knew things weren't going to be like they'd been before. And I knew I couldn't change that. I had to find peace with that and change the things I could change."

"I planted him a tree," I said, "as my special way of remembering him."

Ms. Gwen smiled at me. "I'm proud of you."

Transitions

When I got home from school that first day, Ma was packing some things to take to the hospital. I had something I needed to do before we left.

I walked to the kitchen and heated some water in the microwave. Then I mixed in some oatmeal flakes. Buttons sat at my feet watching my every move.

I held the bowl in my hand as I opened the back door. Buttons followed right along. I looked at the trees in the backyard. White flowers bloomed on the green hawthorn, and the live oak, though still fragile, looked full of life.

Pop would've adored seeing the trees. I thought of his name. Alfred. My father. I miss you, Pop.

I took a wad of moist oatmeal. It made a "whap" as it hit the live oak's stake. Buttons sniffed at what dropped to the ground.

I laughed. As crazy as that sounds, I laughed. A thick and hearty laugh I hoped sounded like my father's.

I wanted to share a memory with him, even though he wasn't home quite yet.

"What on earth are you doing?" Ma asked as she approached me from behind.

I laughed again. "Thinking of Pop," I said.

She paused for a moment. Then Ma stuck her hand in the gooey oatmeal and tossed a ball at the base of the green hawthorn. She missed and hit a branch instead. A handful of five-petal flowers fell to the ground.

"Did you notice anything when you got home?" Ma asked. "No," I said. I hadn't noticed anything.

"Go look out front," Ma said, flicking some oatmeal chunks off her hand.

When I got to the front, I realized right away what was missing. The For Sale sign.

A Flower for Me

"I can't leave what your father and I worked our whole lives for," Ma said as she joined me in the front yard. "When he gets out of the hospital, I want him to be able to come home. To this home," she said, her voice shaky.

"Trudy, we're going through a transition, a major transition, in our life. I'm going to need your help. We have to make something good out of the bad."

Minutes passed before she spoke again.

"I don't know what's going to happen," Ma continued. "I guess only time will tell. All we can do is go forward."

I nodded my head in agreement.

"Just know how much he loves you, Trudy. How much I love you. Know that whatever happens, that will never change."

"Do you think he . . ." I murmured before I started to cry.

Ma knew what I wanted to ask.

"Yes," she said, "he knows how much you love him. There's no doubt about that."

That night, I studied the gift Pop had given me. One of the flowers had begun to open, revealing a white iris with touches of violet in the center. All around me I felt Pop's love and a hope for tomorrow.

Jessica Lee Anderson lives in Austin, Texas, with her husband, Michael, and Buster, their Yorkshire "Terror." While her experiences have ranged from teaching and selling computers to coordinating a vision therapy clinic, her lifelong passion is writing literature for children.

If you enjoyed this book, you'll also want to read these other Milkweed novels.

To order books or for more information, contact Milkweed at (800) 520-6455 or visit our Web site (www.milkweed.org).

The $66 Summer
John Armistead

Milkweed Prize for Children's Literature
New York Public Library Best Books of the Year: "Books for the Teen Age"

A story of interracial friendships in the segregation-era South.

The Return of Gabriel
John Armistead

A story of Freedom Summer.

The Ocean Within
V. M. Caldwell

Milkweed Prize for Children's Literature

Focuses on an older child adopted into a large, extended family.

Tides
V. M. Caldwell

The sequel to *The Ocean Within*, this book deals with the troubles of older siblings.

Alligator Crossing
Marjory Stoneman Douglas

Features the wildlife of the Everglades just before it was declared a national park.

Perfect
Natasha Friend

Milkweed Prize for Children's Literature

A thirteen-year-old girl struggles with bulimia after her father dies.

Parents Wanted
George Harrar

Milkweed Prize for Children's Literature

Focuses on the adoption of a boy with ADD.

The Trouble with Jeremy Chance
George Harrar

Bank Street College Best Children's Books of the Year

Father-son conflict during the final days of World War I.

No Place
Kay Haugaard

Based on a true story of Latino youth who create an inner-city park.

The Monkey Thief
Aileen Kilgore Henderson

New York Public Library Best Books of the Year: "Books for the Teen Age"

A twelve-year-old boy is sent to live with his uncle in a Costa Rican rain forest.

Hard Times for Jake Smith
Aileen Kilgore Henderson

A girl searches for her family in the Depression-era South.

The Summer of the Bonepile Monster
Aileen Kilgore Henderson

Milkweed Prize for Children's Literature

A brother and sister spend the summer with their great-grandmother in the South.

Treasure of Panther Peak
Aileen Kilgore Henderson

New York Public Library Best Books of the Year: "Books for the Teen Age"

A twelve-year-old girl adjusts to her new life in Big Bend National Park.

I Am Lavina Cumming
Susan Lowell

Mountains & Plains Booksellers
Association Award

This lively story culminates with the 1906
San Francisco earthquake.

The Boy with Paper Wings
Susan Lowell

This story about a feverish boy's imagined
battles includes paper-folding instructions.

The Secret of the Ruby Ring
Yvonne MacGrory

A blend of time travel and historical fiction
set in 1885 Ireland.

Emma and the Ruby Ring
Yvonne MacGrory

A tale of time travel to nineteenth-century
Ireland.

A Bride for Anna's Papa
Isabel R. Marvin

Milkweed Prize for Children's Literature

Life on Minnesota's Iron Range in the early
1900s.

Minnie
Annie M. G. Schmidt

A cat turns into a woman and helps a hapless newspaperman.

A Small Boat at the Bottom of the Sea
John Thomson

Donovan's Puget Sound summer with his ailing aunt and mysterious uncle tests his convictions when he suspects his uncle is involved with shady characters.

The Dog with Golden Eyes
Frances Wilbur

Milkweed Prize for Children's Literature

A young girl's dream of owning a dog comes true, but it may be more than she's bargained for.

Behind the Bedroom Wall
Laura E. Williams

Milkweed Prize for Children's Literature
Jane Addams Peace Award Honor Book

Tells a story of the Holocaust through the eyes of a young girl.

The Spider's Web
Laura E. Williams

A young girl in a neo-Nazi group sets off a chain of events when she's befriended by an old German woman.

Milkweed Editions

Founded in 1979, Milkweed Editions is the largest independent, nonprofit literary publisher in the United States. Milkweed publishes with the intention of making a humane impact on society, in the belief that good writing can transform the human heart and spirit. Within this mission, Milkweed publishes in five areas: fiction, nonfiction, poetry, children's literature for middle-grade readers, and the World As Home—books about our relationship with the natural world.

Join Us

Milkweed depends on the generosity of foundations and individuals like you, in addition to the sales of its books. In an increasingly consolidated and bottom-line–driven publishing world, your support allows us to select and publish books on the basis of their literary quality and the depth of their message. Please visit our Web site (www.milkweed.org) or contact us at (800) 520-6455 to learn more about our donor program.

Interior design and typesetting by Dorie McClelland
Typeset in ITC Berekeley, Tiki Holiday, and Gill Sans
Printed on acid-free 55 lb. Eco Book Natural Cream paper
by Friesens Corporation